THE IMPORTANCE OF

George W. Bush

These and other titles are included in The Importance Of biography series:

Maya Angelou
Louis Armstrong
Neil Armstrong
Lucille Ball
The Beatles
Alexander Graham Bell
Napoleon Bonaparte
Fidel Castro
Leonardo da Vinci
James Dean
Walt Disney
F. Scott Fitzgerald
Henry Ford
Anne Frank
Mohandas Gandhi
John Glenn
Martha Graham
Ernest Hemingway
Henry VIII
Adolf Hitler
Thomas Jefferson
John F. Kennedy

Bruce Lee
Lenin
John Lennon
Abraham Lincoln
Charles Lindbergh
Paul McCartney
Mother Teresa
Muhammad
John Muir
Richard Nixon
Pablo Picasso
Edgar Allan Poe
Queen Elizabeth I
Jonas Salk
Margaret Sanger
Dr. Seuss
William Shakespeare
Frank Sinatra
J.R.R. Tolkien
Simon Wiesenthal
The Wright Brothers

THE IMPORTANCE OF

George W. Bush

by Corinne J. Naden and Rose Blue

San Diego • Detroit • New York • San Francisco • Cleveland • New Haven, Conn. • Waterville, Maine • London • Munich

CODMAN SQUARE

JAN 2005

© 2004 by Lucent Books. Lucent Books is an imprint of The Gale Group, Inc., a division of Thomson Learning, Inc.

Lucent Books® and Thomson Learning™ are trademarks used herein under license.

For more information, contact
Lucent Books
27500 Drake Rd.
Farmington Hills, MI 48331-3535
Or you can visit our Internet site at http://www.gale.com

ALL RIGHTS RESERVED.
No part of this work covered by the copyright hereon may be reproduced or used in any form or by any means—graphic, electronic, or mechanical, including photocopying, recording, taping, Web distribution, or information storage and retrieval systems—without the written permission of the publisher.

LIBRARY OF CONGRESS CATALOGING-IN-PUBLICATION DATA

Blue, Rose.
　George W. Bush / by Rose Blue and Corinne J. Naden.
　p. cm. — (The importance of)
　　ISBN 1-59018-282-0
　　1. Bush, George W. (George Walker), 1946—Juvenile literature. 2. Presidents—United States—Biography—Juvenile literature. I. Naden, Corinne J. II. Title. III. Series
　　E903.B58 2004
　　973.931'092—dc22

2004000383

Printed in the United States of America

Contents

Foreword	7
INTRODUCTION *Terror Hits Home*	8
CHAPTER 1 *A Strong Family Bond*	13
CHAPTER 2 *Later School Years*	24
CHAPTER 3 *The Businessman from Texas*	36
CHAPTER 4 *In the Governor's Seat*	48
CHAPTER 5 *The Disputed Election*	59
CHAPTER 6 *Policy at Home and Abroad*	70
CHAPTER 7 *Justifying War*	81
EPILOGUE *The Next Journey*	93
Notes	97
For Further Reading	99
Works Consulted	101
Index	103
Picture Credits	111
About the Authors	112

Foreword

THE IMPORTANCE OF biography series deals with individuals who have made a unique contribution to history. The editors of the series have deliberately chosen to cast a wide net and include people from all fields of endeavor. Individuals from politics, music, art, literature, philosophy, science, sports, and religion are all represented. In addition, the editors did not restrict the series to individuals whose accomplishments have helped change the course of history. Of necessity, this criterion would have eliminated many whose contribution was great, though limited. Charles Darwin, for example, was responsible for radically altering the scientific view of the natural history of the world. His achievements continue to impact the study of science today. Others, such as Chief Joseph of the Nez Percé, played a pivotal role in the history of their own people. While Joseph's influence does not extend much beyond the Nez Percé, his nonviolent resistance to white expansion and his continuing role in protecting his tribe and his homeland remain an inspiration to all.

These biographies are more than factual chronicles. Each volume attempts to emphasize an individual's contributions both in his or her own time and for posterity. For example, the voyages of Christopher Columbus opened the way to European colonization of the New World. Unquestionably, his encounter with the New World brought monumental changes to both Europe and the Americas in his day. Today, however, the broader impact of Columbus's voyages is being critically scrutinized. *Christopher Columbus*, as well as every biography in The Importance Of series, includes and evaluates the most recent scholarship available on each subject.

Each author includes a wide variety of primary and secondary source quotations to document and substantiate his or her work. All quotes are footnoted to show readers exactly how and where biographers derive their information, as well as provide stepping-stones to further research. These quotations enliven the text by giving readers eyewitness views of the life and times of each individual covered in The Importance Of series.

Finally, each volume is enhanced by photographs, bibliographies, chronologies, and comprehensive indexes. For both the casual reader and the student engaged in research, The Importance Of biographies will be a fascinating adventure into the lives of people who have helped shape humanity's past and present, and who will continue to shape its future.

Introduction

Terror Hits Home

When foreign terrorists attacked the United States on September 11, 2001, destroying the World Trade Center in New York City and severely damaging the Pentagon in Washington, D.C., Americans looked for leadership from a president they hardly knew. In those few hours after the tragedy, George W. Bush began to emerge as a man the people felt they could rely on.

On the morning of September 11, 2001, Bush had been president of the United States for nearly nine months. During a good part of that time, the country was squabbling over whether he should even be president. He had not won the popular vote, losing that to Al Gore by a count of 51,003,894 to 50,459,211. Some people were not even certain he had won the electoral vote (271 to 266) because of the dispute in the state of Florida over voting machines and the vote count. In any event, the new president was not very visible in those first months in office.

However, on September 11, most people forgot the election and almost everything else for awhile. At 8:45 A.M. eastern standard time, American Airlines Flight 11 out of Boston, Massachusetts, crashed into the north tower of the World Trade Center's twin skyscrapers in New York City. The plane had been hijacked. Eighteen minutes later, a second plane—United Airlines Flight 175, also from Boston—crashed into the south tower and exploded.

Now, both towers were burning. At 9:21 A.M., all New York City airports were ordered closed and all tunnels and bridges shut down. This was followed by an order to close all airports all over the country—the first time that had ever happened in U.S. history.

At 9:43 A.M. another hijacked American Airlines plane crashed into the Pentagon building in Washington, D.C., causing great structural damage. At 10:05 A.M., the Trade Center's 110-story south tower collapsed. Tons of glass, concrete, and steel tumbled down to the city streets below. At 10:10 A.M., a fourth hijacked plane, this one belonging to United Airlines, crashed in a field near Pittsburgh, Pennsylvania. Also about that time, part of the Pentagon building collapsed. And at 10:28 A.M., the Trade Center's north tower began to fall. Thousands of people were feared dead.

When news of the attacks first reached George W. Bush, he was speaking in Sarasota, Florida, but immediately left the state on *Air Force One,* the presidential plane. He was next heard from at 1:04 P.M. speaking from Barksdale Air Force Base in Louisiana from where he told the American people that all security measures possible were being taken. He assured the public that those responsible for the terrorism would be punished. Then he was hustled back onto *Air Force One.*

For the next few hours, the public wondered where the president was. Then, at 3:55 P.M., a White House aide went on air to report that Bush was now at Offutt Air Force Base in Nebraska where he was conducting a National Security Council meeting by phone. Vice President Dick Cheney and National Security Adviser Condoleezza Rice were at a secure site in the White House. Defense Secretary Donald Rumsfeld was at the Pentagon.

By 4:30 P.M., the president was in the air again to return to Washington. He was back at the White House by 7 P.M. and went on the air nationwide at 8:30 P.M.

Chief of Staff Andrew Card informs President George W. Bush of the September 11, 2001, terrorist attacks. Bush responded to the news with resolve to punish those responsible.

Although Bush was visibly shaken following the terrorist attacks, he delivered several television addresses to help reassure the American people.

By this time, the American people had plenty of reasons to be jittery. U.S. Secret Service agents armed with automatic rifles were patrolling the streets outside the White House. Some eleven thousand people had been evacuated from the United Nations buildings in New York. All flights coming into the United States were being sent to Canada. Two U.S. aircraft carriers had left Norfolk, Virginia, to protect the East Coast in case of further attack. The forty-seven-story Building 7 of the World Trade Center complex had also collapsed. Downtown New York was burning or littered with rubble. The toll of dead office workers, police officers, and firefighters in the Trade Center was mounting.

A noticeably nervous George W. Bush spoke of the "thousands of lives suddenly ended by evil," and said, "These acts shattered steel, but they cannot dent the steel of American resolve."[1] He told Americans that the government would find and punish those responsible. To underscore that the country was in operating condition, he said that all government workers would be back on the job the next day. However, the president did not show any anger or give any particular indication of what steps the government would take following this shock and tragedy.

Over the next few days, the number of deaths and casualties mounted. (As of late 2003, the official death toll from the World Trade Center collapse reached 2,752.) The American people began to get used to the sight of the president. He was frequently seen at the White House meeting with government officials. He inspected the shattered Pentagon building and, three days after the attack, met with New York City's mayor Rudolph Giuliani at the ruins of the World Trade Center, now being called Ground Zero.

Looking for a sign of reassurance, people lined the streets and cheered as he drove past accompanied by Giuliani. As though showing the president how times had changed since the tragedy, the mayor said to him, "You see those people cheering you? Not one of them voted for you."[2] (New York State had voted for Al Gore by a large margin.)

On the night of the terrorist attack, Bush had spoken to the nation without

Three days after the attacks, President Bush toured the site of the World Trade Center. Here, he speaks to firefighters at Ground Zero.

anger or resolution and with visible jitteriness. In the ensuing days, he had allowed anger to creep into his voice, and his sense of steely resolve began to show. It was as though he was accepting the authority of his office.

But in accepting this authority, in the following months, Bush redefined the presidency as well. He became the first U.S. president in history to launch a preemptive war—against Iraq in 2003—and in so doing changed the role of America in the world as well as other nations' view of that role. He also charged ahead with his own policies with disregard for world—and in some cases his constituents'—opinion. He declares he governs as a compassionate conservative, a philosophy that deems it compassionate to help people and conservative to insist on accountability and results. This philosophy governs all his decisions as the chief executive. For better or worse, Bush has changed the role of the presidency.

Chapter 1

A Strong Family Bond

George W. Bush was born into a wealthy family whose close personal ties withstood sorrow and disappointment and whose strength became a major factor in his life. A love of politics is the second strong bond that holds this very political family together.

PROGRAMMED FOR SUCCESS

George Walker Bush was born on July 6, 1946, in New Haven, Connecticut, into a family whose members included a number of distinguished achievers. His paternal grandfather, Prescott Sheldon Bush, graduated from Yale University in 1917, joined the Connecticut National Guard, and was part of the American Expeditionary Forces in World War II. After military service, he began a successful career in banking and lost a run at a U.S. Senate seat in 1950. He did, however, win the election two years later, serving until 1961.

Bush's father, George Herbert Walker Bush, attended the prestigious Phillips Academy prep school in Andover, Massachusetts. After graduation, he entered the military in 1943 on his eighteenth birthday and became the youngest pilot in the U.S. Navy. He returned home in 1945, married Barbara Pierce, and entered Yale University, where he studied economics.

Bush's mother, Barbara Pierce Bush, was born in New York City and grew up in the well-to-do community of Rye, New York, about twenty-five miles northeast of the city. Her father was a magazine publisher and president of the McCall Corporation. One of four children, she attended public school in Rye for six years and then entered the private Rye Country Day School. She graduated from Ashley Hall, an all-girls high school in Charleston, South Carolina, then enrolled at Smith College in Massachusetts, which she left after her marriage to Bush's father.

When Bush was born, World War II was ending, and his parents were trying to adjust to civilian life. George was their first child. The family often called him "Little George." His mother frequently called him "George Junior," although that is not his name. People say he inherited his looks from his father and his sense of humor, as well as his blunt way of speaking, from his mother.

Bush's father George Herbert Walker Bush spent three years in the military, where he achieved the rank of lieutenant and became the youngest pilot in the U.S. Navy.

The Family Bush

After the elder Bush graduated from Yale in 1948, he moved the family to Odessa, Texas. Neil Mallon, a long-time friend of Prescott Bush, had offered him a job as a trainee at International Derrick and Equipment Company, a subsidiary of Dresser Industries, an oil conglomerate in which the Bush family had investments. Mallon was the head of Dresser.

George W. Bush was too young to remember, but his father recalls on arriving in Texas in his new red Studebaker that "moving from New Haven to Odessa just about the day I graduated was quite a shift in lifestyle."[3] A working-class town in west Texas, Odessa featured few trees and what seemed to be endless sandstorms. There were so many, in fact, that they were given names, much as hurricanes are named today. Bush's mother remembers that they had the only refrigerator on the block. For a short time in 1949, the family moved to California where the senior Bush was a drill-bit salesman, but they returned to Texas in time for the birth of their second child, daughter Pauline Robinson, named for Mrs. Bush's mother and called Robin.

The family settled down not in Odessa but in nearby Midland. It was a decided step up in living style. A Texas saying went, "You raised hell in Odessa, you raised your family in Midland."[4] The Bush family moved into a new neighborhood of pastel-colored, wooden bungalows, each seven thousand five hundred dollars and each exactly the same. There were still no trees, but young George was happy because there were lots of kids to play with.

In 1950, the elder Bush and John Overbey, an oil and gas broker in Midland, formed the Bush-Overbey Oil Development Corporation. They believed it was just a matter of time before the oil boom, which was developing elsewhere in Texas, would reach the western part of the state. Their idea was to buy and sell oil-drilling rights in the area. In the meantime, young George was settling down to life in west Texas, busy with school, play, and friends and attending Sunday school at First Presbyterian Church.

A Time of Sadness

In early 1953, a third child and second son joined the Bush family. John Ellis (called Jeb for his initials) was born, and just about that time, three-year-old Robin began to complain of being tired. She refused to play and just wanted to stay in bed. Her parents took her to the doctor, who had some blood tests performed. The diagnosis was shocking. The little girl had leukemia, a cancer of the blood that in those days was nearly always fatal.

Robin was taken to Memorial Sloan-Kettering Hospital in New York City, famed for its cancer treatment. John Walker, the elder Bush's uncle, was president of the hospital. Bush's mother stayed with Robin at the hospital and his father flew up on weekends. During the week, relatives and friends cared for the other children. Robin lived for eight months and died in 1953. Young George had not been told of the severity of his sister's condition. He was in the second grade at Midland's Sam Houston Elementary School at the time and her death came as a severe shock.

Barbara Bush later said that she could not get over her own depression until, as she recalled,

> George Junior saved my life. I spent a lot of time playing with him and with Jebby after Robin's death, but I didn't realize that George Junior was humoring me until I heard him tell a playmate that he couldn't come out today because he had to play with his mother, who was lonely. You have to remember that children grieve. At first George Junior couldn't believe she had died and was buried. He felt cheated. I'm not sure George and I handled it as well as we should have.[5]

Bush himself later said of that period, "Mother's reaction was to envelop herself totally around me. She kind of smothered me and then recognized that it was the wrong thing to do."[6] However, young George and his mother emerged from that terrible period with a special and close bond.

School Days

Bush says, "If you really want to understand someone, you look at his family and where he was raised."[7] He and his siblings grew up in a close, competitive, laughter-filled home. He remembers that his father was not always around as much as he would have liked due to business and, later, politics, but his mother kept a strict eye and hand on the group. Sometimes George and Barbara Bush would go to New York or to the family estate in Connecticut, leaving young George and his siblings in the care of two regular maids. One of them said that "Little George and his mother were always colliding because they were together so much . . . and because they were so much alike. They would squabble a lot. . . . He was definitely like his mother, they were exactly alike, even their humor was alike."[8]

At Sam Houston Elementary School, George W. was a decent student who got into his share of mischief. In the third grade, he threw a football out of a school window because it was raining and no one could go out to play at lunchtime. He also used to brag that he had a swimsuit on under his blue jeans. (By that time, the elder Bush was doing well enough in the oil business to move the family into a new brick home complete with swimming pool and cabana.) In the fourth grade, George W. was sent to the principal's office for painting his face with a ballpoint pen. The long sideburns indicated that he wanted to look like Elvis Presley. Teachers remembered him as a bit cocky but fun loving.

George W. may not have been an A student in the classroom, but he had a knack for memorizing figures, such as baseball stats. As a grade-school youngster, he set himself the task of memorizing the starting lineups of every major league baseball team. He began playing baseball and

The Youngest Hero

George Herbert Walker Bush, President George W. Bush's father, was not only a pilot during World War II, but, at eighteen years old, he was the U.S. Navy's youngest pilot. Although he joined the service right out of high school as a seaman second class, he qualified for flight school. He was assigned to the VT-51 torpedo bomber squadron and flew fifty-eight missions in a three-man, single-engine Grumman Avenger off the aircraft carrier *San Jacinto* in the Pacific. He was one of only four pilots to survive the war out of his original fourteen-pilot squadron.

His second most harrowing day occurred on June 19, 1944, when he was forced to land at sea and narrowly escaped before his plane exploded. He was picked up by a U.S. ship in half an hour. His most harrowing day was on September 2, 1944, on a bombing mission against the Japanese-held Bonin Islands when his plane was hit by enemy aircraft fire. He managed to drop his bombs on the target and head out to sea. His tailgunner was already dead and his radioman died when he parachuted out of the plane. Bush jumped and slammed into the tail of the plane, injuring his scalp and ripping his parachute. But he splashed down safely, got into a rubber life raft, and spent three long hours bobbing about until the U.S. submarine *Finback* rescued him. For that adventure, Bush received the Distinguished Flying Cross.

---

football as soon as he was old enough. Between the ages of nine and thirteen, he played baseball for the Midland Central Little League Cubs and played sandlot football as well. When he attended San Jacinto Junior High in Midland, he played both baseball and football. His father took him to football games at Yale when he was just an infant and later taught him how to pitch and catch in the backyard in Texas. The younger Bush never became a talented player in any sport, but he loved to play, and he was always enthusiastic about it.

Bush recalls a happy childhood of playing games and fooling around with friends. He was well liked and friendly, and always seemed at ease with older people. But even though west Texas was his home and the young boy fit in, his family was somewhat different from their neighbors. For one thing, they made regular journeys to the Bush family home in Kennebunkport, Maine. Most of the Bush relatives had made their money in Wall Street, and they eagerly listened to the tales of spouting oil wells and life in the Texas desert from the western side of the family.

Changing Location

As Bush grew, so did the Bush family. Neil was born in 1955, Marvin in 1956,

Bush's mother Barbara Pierce came from an affluent suburban New York family. She and his father married in 1945.

and Dorothy in 1959. Except for somewhat frequent fistfights between George and his brothers, invariably broken up by their mother, the Bush children got along well.

Soon after Robin died, the elder Bush had entered into a new venture, the Zapata Petroleum Corporation, which drilled new oil wells. At about the time Dorothy was born, the oil boom in west Texas was dwindling. The elder Bush decided it was time to try drilling offshore in the Gulf of Mexico.

Finding it impossible to run an offshore business from Midland, the elder Bush transplanted the family to Houston in the southeastern part of the state in 1959. The Bush family moved into a home that was custom designed by an architect to fit their needs and lifestyle. It contained not only a swimming pool but also a small baseball field. It was also built on a huge plot of land.

The move to Houston was intended to aid the elder Bush's oil business, but it was a socially comfortable change as well. Houston was an energetic, multicultural, socially busy city that was in many ways comparable to life in the northeast as George and Barbara Bush had known it. It was also a place of political opportunity, which was of interest to the elder Bush.

Once the family settled in Houston, George W., who was now thirteen years old, was ready for the eighth grade. So far, he had attended public schools, but for some time, George's parents had been talking about whether to send him to a private school. They decided he would benefit from the environment, so he was enrolled for the eighth and ninth grades at The Kinkaid School in Houston,

SAM HOUSTON'S CITY

When George W. Bush was thirteen, the family moved to Houston, the largest metropolis in the state of Texas—an inland port city named for the first president of the Republic of Texas, Sam Houston. It was founded in 1836 by New York brothers and land speculators Augustus C. Allen and John K. Allen, who placed an ad saying the site was a future inland bonanza for the businessman. John Allen actually persuaded the first Congress of the Republic of Texas to move there later that year, but the government stayed only until 1839. Legislators were reportedly tired of walking around in mud and suffering from yellow-fever epidemics. The average summer temperature is ninety-three degrees.

Houston grew slowly as a cotton port, then developed as a railroad center. When oil was discovered in 1901 at the famous Spindletop gusher just outside of town, the oil boom began. Because of the great resources in oil, natural gas, sulfur, lime, salt, and water in the area, a great concentration of industry slowly grew along the coast.

considered to be one of the state's most exclusive.

Even though he had come from a small school in Midland, George W. fit in very well at Kinkaid. He was popular, a class officer, and an admired sports star, mostly in baseball. His teachers remembered him as good looking, intense, and someone who joined in, especially on the debate team.

During his Kinkaid years, George W. and his mother grew even closer. His father was often away from home for long periods tending to the prospering oil business. The elder Bush was also taking an interest in Republican Party affairs. He had campaigned in Midland for Dwight D. Eisenhower for president in 1952 and 1956. When her husband was away, Barbara Bush was alone much of the time with five children to care for. Although just a young teenager, George W. seemed older than his years, and Barbara often leaned on him for emotional comfort.

During his summer vacations, Bush was sent to Camp Longhorn near Austin, Texas. The camp was run by a former Olympic swimmer and water polo player, Julian William "Tex" Robertson from Michigan. Wealthy families sent their children to Longhorn. It was a supervised, healthy environment for energetic teenagers and the setting for endless and spirited physical competition. Coming from a family of competitors, including his own siblings, George W. was a natural for the camp. He cheerfully endured such moments as making an icy plunge into Inks Lake to swim the traditional required mile. And he was given Longhorn's most coveted honor—Campfire Lighter. Only the best campers were given the honor of lighting the campfire each night.

When Bush's father returned from business trips, there were often backyard barbecues or other social events at the Bush home. Doug Hannah, a young friend and neighbor in Houston, remembered spending time with Bush. Hannah often had to wait for his friend to come out to enjoy a Saturday afternoon because his mother was holding up flash cards for new vocabulary words that her son had to learn that weekend. He also remembered that the Bush family was different than others in Houston, mostly because their house was so often filled with people from Connecticut or New York, and if the topic of conversation was not oil, it was business or politics.

Hannah recalled that even at that young age, George W. was becoming political. He said that Bush "seemed to be directly emulating his father, winding his way from one side of the party to the other, mingling, shaking hands, making sure he said hello to everyone in the room when he walked in, making sure to say good-bye to everyone on the way out." Hannah said that Bush "has always been a political person. He would walk in that room and work it. Even as an eighth-grader, and that's pretty foreign to a juvenile to even think that that is important."[9]

LIKE FATHER, LIKE SON

Bush was following his father in his early interest in politics. But unlike his father, he was growing up with firm Texas roots.

George W. (left center) enjoyed a happy childhood as the firstborn in a large family. As a child, Bush was popular with his peers.

A STRONG FAMILY BOND

The elder Bush (left) was captain of the baseball team at Phillips Academy, a prestigious school in Andover, Massachusetts. In 1961 the Bushes enrolled their son at the academy.

Now, to broaden his academic experience, his family decided that he should spend the next few years in the northeast, in the same prep school where the elder Bush had been educated.

The Bushes sent their eldest son to Phillips Academy (known as Andover) in Andover, Massachusetts. He was accepted in 1961 at the age of fifteen. A cousin later said that Bush did not particularly want to go to Andover, nor even to leave Texas, but he went along with his parents' wishes.

Bush's experiences at Andover in the 1960s were greatly different from his school years in Texas. Life at the academy was very structured, much like a military school. The young men wore coats and ties, reported for breakfast early, and then went to required chapel, receiving demerits for being even seconds late. Classes

22 ■ THE IMPORTANCE OF GEORGE W. BUSH

ended early in the afternoon, followed by two hours of sports activities. Then it was back to the schoolroom until 6:00 P.M. Students were allowed just seven minutes between classes.

In 1962, *Time* magazine carried an article on Andover, calling it the hardest school in the country. Clay Johnson from Fort Worth, Texas, a classmate at Andover, recalled, "There was an article about private schools in *Time* magazine our first or second year. The headmaster of Andover was on the cover, and the point was that Andover was the hardest school in the country. I remember reading that and thinking, 'Oh my God, I'm at the hardest school in the country!' I mean, I thought it was hard, but I didn't realize it was that hard."[10]

Never an outstanding student, Bush had trouble academically at Andover from the start. He did manage to earn average grades his first year despite problems with English and mathematics. In one English class, he was told to write about an experience that was emotional for him. So he looked up the word "tears" in the thesaurus and chose "lacerates." According to an article in *Texas Monthly*, he wrote, "'Lacerates ran down my cheeks.' The professor gave him a zero, calling his paper 'disgraceful.'"[11]

Bush may have had trouble in the classroom, but he had no trouble making friends. He was almost immediately one of the most popular students. He was a good if not outstanding athlete, playing varsity baseball and basketball and junior varsity football. Most of his classmates remember him as a blur of physical activity, ever on the go, always involved in something. He once organized a school stickball league. When he did not make the varsity football team, he became its cheerleader.

There was a great desire at the academy to win the white sweater of an Andover cheerleader, and the competition to join the squad was intense. More than half the boys who tried out for the squad never made it. But Bush was chosen for the honor and even made head cheerleader. He not only headed the squad, but with his natural competitiveness put new pep into the cheers for Andover.

Bush was also elected a representative at-large to the Andover Student Congress. He put new pep into that group, too. Under his lead, the members organized skits that poked fun at students and faculty alike. In prep school, Bush moved easily among his peers, attracting friends with his humor and mostly lighthearted attitude. However, although he later claimed that his years at Andover were invaluable to his career, he also once said that the whole atmosphere of being in the northeast away from Texas was a strange experience for him.

Chapter 2: Later School Years

Despite an undistinguished academic career, George W. Bush was emerging as an affable, well-liked personality who attracted people to him. That had been true from his elementary school years, and it continued into the years that prepared him for a life in government and politics.

During his summers at Andover and before going to college, Bush worked at various jobs arranged for by the family and intended to broaden his experience. He did odd jobs at a Houston law office, and one year he was sent to the Quarter Circle XX Ranch in northern Arizona, about thirty miles west of Flagstaff. The ranch was owned by John Greenway, a U.S. senator, and his wife, Isabella, a member of the House. Their son Jack and the elder Bush had been roommates at Andover. That summer was quite a challenge for a teenager without experience with workhorses. He was put to work on a 224-square-mile spread on a seven-thousand-foot-high mountain. For two hundred dollars a month, he helped to build fences and corral cattle. Most of the ranch hands seemed to like the young man. Bush himself said little of the experience except that he did not much like rattlesnakes.

The Acceptance

After graduating from Andover and surviving work on a southwestern ranch, Bush was ready for college. Because his father had gone to Yale from Andover, and because his grandfather had gone to Yale, Bush expected to go to Yale, too. When he had told the dean at Andover of his intention, the dean quietly suggested he look elsewhere. It did not seem possible that Bush's grades could get him into the Ivy League college. Just to be on the safe side, Bush applied to the University of Texas and told everyone that he did not really care about going to Yale.

Thirty students made it to Yale from Andover in 1964; Bush was one of the thirty. Classmates remembered that he truly seemed overjoyed. Through the years, there have been rumors that the right connections eased Bush's acceptance into Yale, although he has always claimed otherwise.

The Elder Bush in Politics

Before Bush entered Yale in the fall of 1964, he spent the summer in Houston working for his father's race for the U.S. Senate. The elder Bush had decided to challenge liberal incumbent senator Ralph Yarborough. Bush backed conservative Barry Goldwater who was running on the Republican ticket against the incumbent president, Democrat Lyndon B. Johnson. As vice president, Johnson had taken office upon the assassination of John F. Kennedy in November 1963. Candidate Bush opposed the comprehensive civil rights legislation intended to end discrimination based on race, color, religion, or national origin, passed by Congress in 1964. Both Goldwater and former vice president Richard Nixon traveled to Texas to support Bush in his campaign to unseat the Democrat. Nixon, who had been defeated for the presidency by Kennedy, was aiding in Goldwater's campaign.

This was the first foray by the elder Bush into politics in the state of Texas beyond the confines of Midland and Houston and the first inside look for the younger Bush at a campaign. The race was hotly contested, with Yarborough charging that the elder Bush was not truly a candidate from Texas but actually represented the eastern establishment. Young Bush flew back from Yale to Houston on election night for the returns. His father lost by a crushing three hundred thousand votes. Although the elder Bush conceded that the only one to blame for the loss was himself, his son was driven to tears. According to an oft-repeated story, when Bush returned to Yale, the school's chaplain told him, "I knew your father and your father lost to a better man."[12] After that, all the interest the young Bush had exhibited for politics during his father's campaign seemed to die out.

The elder Bush was more successful when he ran for the House from Texas in 1966. Running as a moderate, he defeated a conservative Democrat with 57 percent of the vote. Richard Nixon and House Minority Leader Gerald Ford went to Texas to campaign for him.

AT YALE

While his father pursued a political career, Bush settled into life at Davenport College, one of the twelve dormitories at Yale. Two of his Andover classmates were there also. As before, he made friends easily and concentrated on getting a passing C in his studies. A friend said, "George was the person who in three months knew the name of everybody and actually knew fifty percent of the class."[13] As his father had done before him, he gained admission to Delta Kappa Epsilon (DKE) fraternity, known as the Dekes. The fraternity was noted for housing athletes and having parties. In fact, it was called the biggest party house on campus. During this time, Bush began to overindulge in alcohol. He was also rather well known as a bad dresser, picking up a t-shirt off the floor to wear or donning a tie and coat with no shirt underneath. As at Andover, he seemed to be everywhere, dashing across campus, introducing himself to people, joining in the fun.

Bush's Yale years coincided with a time of growing campus unrest about the escalating war in Vietnam. There were constant debates among the students about the pros and cons of U.S. involvement.

Cheers for Eli Yale!

After prep school, Bush was admitted to the nation's third oldest university—after Harvard and William and Mary, both founded in 1701. Originally called the Collegiate School, it was moved from Old Saybrook to New Haven, Connecticut, in 1717 and named Yale College, for Elihu Yale, a wealthy British trader and philanthropist. It was renamed Yale University in 1886 and became fully coeducational in 1969, although women had been admitted to the graduate school since 1892.

Yale is considered one of America's most highly rated and prestigious institutes of higher learning, and the school is very selective in its admissions. Its art galleries, the first such in a U.S. university, are extensive, and its library is one of the largest in the nation, boasting some 6 million volumes. Besides George Bush and George W. Bush, presidents William Howard Taft (class of 1878) and Gerald Ford (law school class of 1941) also graduated from Yale.

Bush supported the war. Proud of his father's record in World War II, he thought it an honor to serve in the military.

During this period, Bush continued to follow in the footsteps of his father, doing much the same things his father had done at Yale. One of those things was to get engaged. Although he had never been known to date much, Bush surprised his friends in his junior year by announcing his engagement to Cathryn Wolfman, a Rice University student and a neighbor from Houston. It looked as though Bush would get married at the age of twenty, as the elder Bush had done. At first, the couple planned for the wedding to take place between Bush's junior and senior years, but they kept postponing the event and eventually drifted apart.

In his senior year, Bush joined the secret and exclusive Skull & Bones Society. The club has gained notoriety through the years because it swears its members to secrecy once they enter the mausoleum-like doors behind Jonathan Edwards College. Each year, the initiation, also called a process of dying and being reborn, admits fifteen new members who meet regularly to learn more about each other. The few who speak about it suggest that it is not so much sinister as clubby. The atmosphere of power and privilege—real or imagined—inspires loyalty to one's peers and a sense of good fellowship. Bush's grandfather, father, two uncles, a cousin, and family friend Neil Mallon were all members. At this point, however, despite all his family connections and eastern education, Bush very much regarded himself, and wished to be thought of, a Texan.

Also in his senior year, Bush had some trouble with authorities. He traveled to Princeton University in New Jersey for a football game. It had been many a year since Yale had been victorious over the Princeton Tigers, so when the Yale Bulldogs won the game, down came the goalposts, with Bush right in the middle of the crossbars. He recalled later, "I was escorted to the campus police place, and the guy said, 'Leave town.' So I was once in Princeton, New Jersey, and haven't been back since."[14]

THE WORLD'S MOST SECRETIVE ORGANIZATION

The Skull & Bones Society at Yale, of which Bush became a member, is often called one of the most secretive organizations in the world. Those on the inside simply call it The Order (outsiders are referred to as "vandals") and it was once known as the Brotherhood of Death. All its members take a solemn vow of secrecy. Originally a German order, it was founded in 1833 at Yale by General William Huntington Russell and Alphonso Taft, father of William Howard Taft, the nation's twenty-seventh president.

Members of Skull & Bones are chosen in their junior year at Yale and spend only one year in the society. The organization has ceremonial rites and rules, and members are never happy about others trying to pry into their affairs. Besides Bush, many who became powerful business leaders have been members of Skull & Bones, including Henry Luce, who went on to head the Time-Life publishing corporation.

This building houses Yale's Skull & Bones Society, an exclusive organization whose members take a solemn vow of secrecy.

LATER SCHOOL YEARS 27

Bush attended Yale University, his father's alma mater, from 1964 to 1968. Yale is one of the most highly regarded institutions of higher learning in the United States.

GRADUATION AND THE GUARD

In 1968, Bush graduated from Yale and his father was reelected without opposition to the House. It was a turbulent time on college campuses all over the land. The war in Vietnam was dividing the country, which was already reeling from a series of tragedies that decade: John F. Kennedy had been assassinated in 1963. A civil rights bill was passed in 1964, but the fight for equality raged on. Civil rights leader Martin Luther King Jr. was assassinated in

April 1968. Kennedy's brother Robert was shot to death after giving a speech in a Los Angeles hotel in June. The growing war in Vietnam was taking center stage in the public mind, and protests against American involvement increased. There were student uprisings at Columbia University in New York City. Young men burned draft cards or fled to Canada to avoid going into the military.

The sky was a slate gray on that June 9 as Bush and 2,401 other Yale graduates received their degrees. There was no commencement address. An antiwar petition was circulated throughout the departing seniors; Bush had not signed it. His father arrived for the graduation but spent only two hours with his son because of his crowded congressional schedule. Bush said to a friend, "My father doesn't have a normal life. I don't have a normal father."[15]

Bush now had a bachelor's degree in history and no idea what to do with his long-term future. The short term was a little more certain. He would become a fighter pilot, just like his father. Earlier in the year, he had flown to Houston for an interview with the Texas Air National Guard. At the time, there were only two openings for flight training. Bush was accepted for one of them.

Over the years, critics have charged that Bush's family connections helped assure his acceptance in the guard, and that Bush entered the guard to avoid serving in Vietnam, since National Guard units were not regularly sent overseas. Bush and others have denied these accusations. "Nobody did anything for him," said Lieutenant Colonel Walter B. Staudt, who interviewed Bush for the guard. "There was no . . . influence on his behalf. Neither his daddy nor anybody else got him into the guard."[16]

After graduation, Bush flew back to Houston to begin training with the 147th fighter group. After a short basic training stint in which he was introduced to military life, he reported for a year's training at Moody Air Force Base in Valdosta, Georgia.

According to the trainees, Valdosta was corrupt, racist, and dry. Except for the training itself, Bush mainly found it boring. However, he did have one unique experience during that time. President Richard Nixon's daughter Tricia needed a dinner date, so a plane was sent to Valdosta to pick up Bush. It was no secret that the elder Bush wanted to move on to the Senate, and this seemed a friendly way to impress the president. Bush himself never talked much about his date with Tricia, except to say that it did not last very long.

Pilot training consisted of a twelve-hour day, half in the classroom and half in the air. One aspect of it was definitely in Bush's favor: pilots were required to memorize the entire makeup of a plane, and Bush had always been good at memorization. The first test was called the initial progress check (IPC). After that, a pilot had to fly with a superior for a final check. Failing that would mean failing the course, which might mean duty in Vietnam. Worse for Bush, such a failure would be humiliating to his father. Although half his group failed the final check, Bush did not.

Bush trained on the F-102 Interceptor at Valdosta and won his National Guard wings on December 2, 1969. He returned to Houston and duty at Ellington Air Force Base. After completing his active duty on June 23, 1970, Bush had to serve four years, as required, in the reserve, flying jets during one weekend a month. Bush claimed that he asked to serve in Vietnam as an F-102 pilot, although critics say that it was already known when he volunteered that the F-102s were slated for retirement from active duty.

TRY AGAIN

In the meantime, the elder Bush had decided to run for the 1970 Senate race from Texas. Bush who was now a lieutenant in the Texas National Guard, joined his father's campaign against opponent Lloyd Bentsen, who also had a son in the guard. Although Nixon once again went to Texas to campaign for him, the elder Bush lost the Senate seat 53 to 47 percent. Since he was now out of the House too, he was now out of government. The elder Bush was only forty-six years old, but his once-promising political career looked bleak. Yet, a month later, Richard Nixon named the elder Bush as the U.S. ambassador to the United Nations.

Bush had a loss of his own that fall, since his grades at Yale cost him admission to the University of Texas business school. Out of school and still without a clear career goal, Bush went to work in early 1971 with Stratford of Texas, an agribusiness founded and owned by Robert Gow, who was a friend of Bush's cousin Ray Walker. Bush was told to put on a coat and tie and become an office trainee. He found it a boring job and stayed less than nine months.

At about the same time, the now twenty-five-year-old toyed with the idea of running for office himself in the Texas House or Senate. When the local press heard of it, this headline appeared in the *Houston Post:* "Legislative Race Eyed by Bush Jr." According to biographer Bill Minutaglio, "The paper had gotten his name wrong in a headline, in the first story ever published about his own political aspirations—he wasn't a Junior."[17] Some weeks later, after Bush had talked the matter over with his father, he abandoned the idea of running. The elder Bush's objection was that his son did not have enough political experience. To address that problem, in the fall of 1972, Bush joined the Senate campaign of Republican from Alabama Winton M. Blount, who lost in November.

TO HARVARD

During the holidays at his family's home that December, Bush got into trouble with his drinking. He took his sixteen-year-old brother, Marvin, out one night and they both got drunk. Driving home, Bush struck some garbage cans in the driveway, which woke up everybody. The family was less than pleased, but when the elder Bush started to speak to Bush about it, son Jeb broke in and told his father that George W. had been accepted at Harvard Business School, to which he had applied at the same time as his application to the

After graduating from Yale, Bush applied to Harvard Business School only to prove he could get in. Bush's father, however, convinced him to attend.

LATER SCHOOL YEARS

University of Texas. Bush said that he really was not planning to go to Harvard, but he just wanted everyone to know that he could get in. His father advised him to reconsider.

Bush did think about it and decided to go, but since he would not enter until the fall of 1973, his father had another idea. Worried about his son's drinking, the elder Bush thought work with the organization called PULL (Professionals United for Leadership) might be a good experience. He might become more responsible if he saw how privileged he was in contrast with others not so fortunate. Located in one of Houston's tougher districts, PULL brought professional athletes and inner-city kids together. Bush later recalled being shocked when he was playing basketball with one of the boys and a gun fell out of the youth's pocket.

Friendly and easygoing, Bush had success working with the boys at PULL. He wore old clothes, drove an old car, and never acted like a wealthy young man even though everyone knew he was. Bush saw more grinding poverty during those few months than he ever had experienced. He left PULL in the fall of 1973 to enter Harvard Business School.

According to later reports from colleagues at the business school—some of whom had known him from Andover and Yale—and from his mother, Harvard made a distinct difference in Bush's life. It gave him direction and instilled some discipline in what was until then a somewhat frivolous life. It was as though he decided that if he were going to do something with himself, now was the time to start.

The coursework in business school was detailed and analytical; fifteen-hundred-word papers were required each week, and attendance at management classes was mandatory. Harvard Business School was not to be taken lightly; not only is it the world's most prestigious, but one out of every ten Fortune 500 organizations—the top firms in the world—are run by its graduates.

ANOTHER BUSH ATTENDS ANDOVER

Phillips Academy—better known as Andover—was founded in 1778 on a hilltop twenty-one miles north of Boston, Massachusetts. Paul Revere designed the school's seal, and among its most famous students are John F. Kennedy Jr., class of 1979; actor Humphrey Bogart, class of 1920; and Samuel F.B. Morse, class of 1805. When Bush attended, Andover was an all-boys school, but it has been coeducational since 1973 when it merged with the adjacent all-girls Abbot Academy. The school is known for its excellent academic program and the diversity of its student body, which today includes students from nearly all the states and twenty-eight foreign countries.

Bush got down to work and graduated from Harvard in June 1975. His father got a new job that year: after leaving the United Nations in 1973, the elder Bush had become chairman of the Republican National Committee and was named chief U.S. liaison in China from 1974 to 1975. He quietly lobbied for the vice presidential spot when Gerald Ford became president on the resignation of Richard Nixon, but Ford chose Nelson Rockefeller instead. In 1975, Ford asked the elder Bush to become director of the Central Intelligence Agency (CIA), the federal organization that gathers intelligence on enemies of the country.

Bush left Harvard and drove home to Texas in his blue 1970 Oldsmobile Cutlass. Before settling down, however, he flew to China with brothers Marvin and Neil and sister Dorothy to visit their parents before the elder Bush returned to Washington and his new job as head of the CIA. After the trip, Bush decided to seek his fortune in his hometown of Midland. It was a good time to enter the oil business, because Texas was experiencing an oil boom again, and like his father, Bush was eager to make a name for himself.

A Change in Lifestyle

Bush went home to Texas where he was not out of place wearing the cowboy boots he liked so much. He liked the protective isolation of west Texas. After moving into a two-room guest cottage on the grounds of a family friend, he set about learning the oil business. First he became a land man, searching court records to find out the ownership of mineral rights. It was not a spectacular living, but he did well and gained a reputation as a competent worker. In his spare time, he jogged and played touch football, much as he had at Yale and Harvard.

Although he did not date a great deal, Bush was considered a very eligible bachelor, and his friends were always trying to fix him up with a date. In August 1977, friends Joe and Jan O'Neill invited him to a backyard barbecue. Their other guest was a rather shy young woman from Austin, a thirty-year-old librarian named Laura Welch.

Welch was born in Midland and had even been in the seventh grade at the same junior high school as Bush. Her father was a builder and her mother a bookkeeper. She grew up quiet and shy, studying for a degree in education at Southern Methodist University. During those years, she began to get caught up in the beginning women's liberation movement and thought of going to law school, but decided that the classroom was really where she wanted to work. After earning a master's degree from the University of Texas at Austin, she settled in that city and became a librarian in the local school system.

The first meeting between Welch and Bush did not seem promising. She was quiet, smart, and bookish. He was talkative, restless, and outgoing. But they liked each other immediately. She calmed him down when he got too rambunctious and he made her quiet life more exciting. He even made her laugh. The evening after

A 1978 political campaign poster features newlyweds George W. and Laura Bush. Bush and Laura married just three months after their first meeting.

The Future First Lady

When Laura Welch accepted George W. Bush's proposal of marriage in 1977, she made one thing clear. Suspecting that a political career was in Bush's future, she made him promise that she would never have to make a political speech on his behalf. Nonetheless, she took that pledge back when she delivered a speech at the Republican National Convention in Philadelphia in 2000.

Laura Bush was born and brought up in Midland, Texas, an only child. She quit working after her marriage to Bush in November 1977. As first lady of Texas, she took up literacy as a cause, which she espouses as the national first lady today.

---

they first met, they played miniature golf. After that, they began spending most of their free time together.

Bush's mother said she immediately knew the relationship was serious. When he visited his parents at their summer place in Kennebunkport, Bush kept calling Welch every few hours. And when he could not get her on the phone, he cut short his Maine visit and flew back to Texas.

Bush's friends say that when he met Welch he was ready to leave his bachelor life and settle down. Welch, who was quite independent despite her quiet demeanor, was ready, too. They became engaged five weeks after they met. And three months after meeting, they married.

The wedding took place on November 6, 1977, at the First Methodist Church in Midland, where Welch's parents still lived. Her cousin and Bush's brothers were ushers, but there were no bridesmaids or groomsmen. About seventy family members and friends attended. The couple had decided on a small wedding; otherwise they would have had to invite hundreds of friends and colleagues, especially from the Bush side. After the wedding, the newlyweds planned a honeymoon in Mexico—but not right away. Bush had decided on a political campaign.

Chapter 3
The Businessman from Texas

As Bush sought to distinguish himself from the career of his increasingly famous father, his marriage and a commitment to religion would help to give him maturity, confidence, and a new sense of direction. Within the next decade, he would not only have a wife, but a family, a new job, a foot in the political door, and a change of direction to his life.

Political Baby Steps

The new Mrs. Bush got a taste of politics early on in her marriage, since the honeymoon was delayed for a political campaign. Even before they met, Bush had hinted that he might make a race for Congress from the 19th Congressional District. Seventy-seven-year-old Democratic incumbent George Mahon had announced that he would not seek reelection after twenty-two terms. Since Bush had almost no political experience and was sure to face a severe uphill battle from any Democratic challenger, his friends were surprised at his intention.

But Bush was determined, and with his new wife by his side and encouragement from his father, he set out to campaign. He ran on a platform favoring the oil industry. Early on, Bush found that his last name could be both an asset and a liability. His father was well liked in Texas, but he had lost campaigns there, and many still considered him eastern establishment rather than Texas blueblood. In addition, the elder Bush was now working to get the Republican nomination for president in 1980, so the son could not appear to be trying to ride into office on his father's coattails. As for Bush himself, he was far from a smooth campaigner and more often sounded like an Ivy League man, which he was, than just one of the guys. It took some work to remember to say "Lubbock," for instance, instead of "Lubbick." However, Bush did prove himself a tireless candidate.

Before he could run against a Democratic opponent, Bush had to defeat fellow Republicans Joseph Hickox and James Reese, the latter proving the more formidable challenger. Reese kept referring to Bush as "Junior" and painting a picture of an interloper, a carpetbagger who had come from the east to dabble in Texas politics. But Reese's strategy did not work, and Bush won the nomination. His Democratic opponent was Kent Hance, who used much the same strategy as had Reese—Bush was an outsider; he did not belong. Bush himself contributed to that image by running political commercials of himself jogging through the streets. Intended to show a vital, youthful candidate full of pep for the job, the picture Bush painted was instead of the ultimate outsider—after all, cowboys do not jog.

Even more damaging to Bush's campaign was an incident just before the election. One of the Bush team had run an ad in the Texas Tech newspaper advertising free beer at a "Bush Bash." The Hance team saw it and realized what harm it could do; it was no secret in west Texas that Bush liked to drink. Encouraging college students to do so—even though Bush said he had not approved the ad—was not taken lightly by the townsfolk.

Whether due to that incident or a combination of factors, Bush lost his first race, as his father and grandfather had done. The margin was 53 to 47 percent. Thinking back to his grandfather's first political loss in 1950 and his father's first loss in 1964, Bush said, "I don't know whether that means members of the Bush family are stubborn or merely persistent."[18]

The loss was not, however, a tragedy for Bush. He had gained some campaign experience. He had learned that he had better loosen up and shed the eastern image if he wanted to win in Texas. A victory would have sent him away to Washington, D.C., but now he would remain where he was known and could plan his political future accordingly. At the moment, though, there were more pressing concerns: he had a wife to support and they both wanted to have a family, so he decided he had better pay some attention to business.

The Bushes honeymooned in Mexico after the political loss, and she stopped working after their return to Texas. From the beginning, they had a traditional relationship, and she decided early on not to discuss political matters with him. She feels that her husband has plenty of other people to give him political advice. However, according to one oft-repeated story, she did give advice once in Bush's very early career. They were driving home from a political rally, and he asked her to be truthful about how his speech went. According to journalist Elizabeth Mitchell, "She told him it hadn't gone very well. He drove the car right into the garage wall, and he never insisted on truthfulness again."[19]

THE OIL BUSINESS

With politics on the back burner, Bush, as his father had done, organized an oil company. He called it Arbusto, which means "bush" in Spanish. He had incorporated the company just before the congressional race, but it did not begin active business until March 1979. The first well that Arbusto put money into came up dry—not unusual in the oil-drilling business.

Bush worked hard to raise capital for the company, even though he had been given a start by family members and connections. His uncle Jonathan, head of an investment firm in New York, helped him to put the company together, and even his grandmother put up twenty-five hundred dollars. Bush traveled through Texas and to New York to raise capital as well. Once again, he seemed to be everywhere, in a constant hurry to get from place to place.

His new company was not the only change occurring in Bush's life. In 1980, his father became vice president of the United States. The elder Bush had campaigned for the presidential nomination, but when it looked like he would be second best once again, he conceded to Ronald Reagan. At the Republican National Convention that year, there was a strong bid for Reagan to choose former president Gerald Ford as his running mate. However, Reagan chose George Herbert Walker Bush. The younger Bush had worried before about appearing to use his father's

When his father (left center) became President Ronald Reagan's (right center) vice president in 1980, Bush temporarily abandoned his own political aspirations.

position for his own gain, so when the ticket of Reagan and Bush defeated the Democratic ticket of Jimmy Carter and Walter Mondale, there could be no thought of the younger Bush getting into politics, at least for the time being.

Another big change for Bush was the prospect of fatherhood. The Bushes were expecting twins in December 1981. As the pregnancy advanced, there were signs of trouble, and it was discovered that Laura was in the early stages of toxemia. This problem causes high blood pressure, blurred vision, and swelling of the face and hands and can be very serious. When Laura's condition grew worse, it was decided to move her to Baylor Hospital in Dallas. Jenna Welch, named for Laura's mother, and Barbara Pierce, named for Bush's mother, were born small but healthy on November 25.

The new father was still working hard to make his oil company prosper, with moderate success. In 1982, hoping to capitalize on the family name to attract new investors, Bush renamed Arbusto the Bush Exploration Company. By the middle of the 1980s, the company had dug nearly one hundred oil wells, but its hits on oil and gas were slightly below the national average.

With the oil business suffering declining profits in general, Bush was willing to listen when he was offered a deal by two Cincinnati investors in February 1984. They headed a new oil-investing firm called Spectrum 7 and felt they could benefit if they incorporated a company with the Bush name and found a man to lead it who knew the Texas oil business. It was a good deal for Bush. His company merged with Spectrum 7, he got more than 1 million shares of stock, and he was named chairman of the new company, for which he was paid seventy-five thousand dollars a year.

Even the Bush name, however, could not spark the new firm in a time of trouble in the oil industry. When the oil-rich nations of the Middle East, disputing among themselves, began offering their oil on the open market, the price of a barrel of oil dropped drastically, and many American firms were faced with bankruptcy. Spectrum 7 was coming close.

Bush knew that a failed business would damage any future runs for public office. Then along came Harken Energy Corporation of Bedford, Texas. Their business was acquiring smaller companies, and although Spectrum 7 was facing shutdown, it had enough prospects to prove profitable when and if oil prices rose. In return for saving Spectrum, Harken could put a vice president's son on its board of directors. The deal was made. Harken took over Spectrum's debts, Bush became a director on Harken's board in 1985, and he was named a consultant in investor relations for two years at a salary of up to $120,000 yearly. In addition, he received more than $500,000 in Harken stock. Harken also agreed to retain some of Spectrum's employees if they agreed to relocate.

Although the financial deal was a good one for Bush, it was still a mark of failure. He had never succeeded at anything on his own.

Getting a New Outlook

Bush had come once again to a point in his business life where he had to make a decision about his future, and changes in his personal life were in store as well. These changes had their roots in the summer of 1985 during a weekend with the family in Kennebunkport, when Bush spent time with Reverend Billy Graham. Bush later described that experience:

> He [Graham] visited my family for a summer weekend in Maine. I saw him preach at the small summer church, St. Ann's by the Sea. We all had lunch on the patio overlooking the ocean. One evening my dad asked Billy to answer questons from a big group of family gathered for the weekend. He sat by the fire and talked. And what he said sparked a change in my heart. I don't remember the exact words. It was more the power of his example. The Lord was so clearly reflected in his gentle and loving demeanor. The next day we walked and talked at Walker's Point, and I knew I was in the presence of a great man. He was like a magnet; I felt drawn to seek something different. He didn't lecture or admonish; he shared warmth and concern. Billy Graham didn't make you feel guilty; he made you feel loved.[20]

Bush said that after that weekend, he went back to Texas and began to read the Bible regularly. He joined a Bible study group. He and his wife were already members of the First Methodist Church of Midland, but now Bush began to take a more active role, participating in many family programs.

The change in religious outlook also led to another great change in Bush's life—his decision to stop drinking. Everyone knew that Bush liked to drink. He never thought of himself as an alcoholic, as he said later, but it was obvious to all that he talked a little louder and got just a little more smart-mouthed when he drank, which was daily. A friend once asked him: "Can you remember a day when you haven't had a beer?"[21] Bush could not. There were also a few times when Bush had had too much to drink and had verbally attacked reporters for writing something derogatory about his father. Some of Bush's friends felt that his drinking would be a severe handicap if and when he ran for public office.

During a weekend in Colorado Springs in 1986, the Bushes and two other couples from Midland were staying at the lavish Broadmoor Hotel. Laura Bush later remembered that her husband grew louder—and what he regarded as funnier—with every drink he took.

The following morning Bush woke up with a gigantic hangover, but he dragged himself out for a morning run. He was in such bad shape that he had to quit and go back to the hotel. Then and there he made a decision. He told his wife that he was not ever going to drink again. A friend thought of the decision in this way: "He looked in the mirror and said, 'Someday, I might embarrass my father. It might get my dad into trouble.' And boy, that was it. That's

After meeting with spiritual leader Reverend Billy Graham (center), Bush strengthened his religious beliefs and became more active in his church.

how high a priority it was. And he never took another drink."[22]

Campaign Time Again

While Bush made changes in his life, his father got ready to run for the job he had always wanted—president of the United States. In 1988, Reagan had served the eight-year presidential limit, and the elder Bush had won his party's nomination. To the consternation of many in his party, he picked the little-qualified junior senator from Indiana, Dan Quayle, as his running mate. The pair opposed the Democratic

The elder Bush and his political strategist Lee Atwater perform together in celebration of Bush's inauguration as the forty-first president in January 1989.

ticket of little-known Michael S. Dukakis, governor of Massachusetts, and Bush's former political opponent, Senator Lloyd Bentsen of Texas. If Bush won the election, he would become the first sitting vice president since Martin Van Buren (1837) to be elected president.

Father wanted son on his campaign team, and with the oil business on the slow side, the younger Bush was ready and willing to assist in whatever way he could. He was immediately given the job of keeping an eye on Lee Atwater, a political consultant and one of his father's most important advisers. The family was not so sure that Atwater was the right person to represent the elder Bush to the public. Bush and Atwater did not much like each other from the start. After one run-in, Atwater commented that perhaps the younger Bush should move up to Washington if he was not pleased with the way the campaign was going. Bush did just that, moving his family to a townhouse in the capital where he assumed the task of making sure the campaign team worked efficiently for his father's victory. The Bushes sold their house in Midland, because they were not sure where they would live after the election.

The presidential election meant almost as much to the son as to the father. The elder Bush had succeeded in just about everything he had really wanted; if he lost this election, his public career was surely over. As his father's biggest fan, Bush longed for a victory. The campaign also gave father and son something they had not had for a long, long time—a chance to be together for extended periods of time.

Once again, Bush was everywhere, dashing about the country, making sure that his father's campaign ran into as few snags as possible. One of his jobs was squelching rumors, including the one that the elder Bush was having an affair with an aide. On that point, Bush dared to confront his father with the question. The elder Bush emphatically denied the rumor and the issue was put down to political dirty tricks.

At the Republican convention in August, Bush was named spokeperson for the Texas delegation. During the last weeks of the campaign, he toured cities in Texas for his father. And on election night, he could be justly proud of his effort when George Herbert Walker Bush became the forty-first president of the United States with 53.4 percent of the popular vote and forty states captured in the electoral college.

After his father's victory, Bush asked a campaign staffer: "What's gonna happen to me?"[23] It was an understandable question. His father was now president of the United States, and although the son still worked as a consultant for Harken, it was not a full-time position. He had no interest in living in Washington, D.C., a city he did not like, but he did not know what he would he do if he returned to Texas.

Bush stayed on in Washington for a few months to help with the transition period. Then he and the family moved back to Texas and bought a home in north Dallas. He still had to earn the consulting fee that Harken was paying him, but the desire to run for public office, even with his father in the White House, was growing. After all, he had sharpened his political skills during his father's reelection campaign. Perhaps it was time for his own entrance into the political sphere.

For some time, Bush had dreamed of running for the governorship of Texas, but he had been out of state affairs for awhile, so he first needed to get back in the public eye. He also needed lots of money to launch a campaign if he chose to run. A baseball team gave him both.

LOOKING FOR A HOME RUN

The Texas Rangers baseball team had been put up for sale before the election in 1988 by the owner, Fort Worth oil baron Eddie Chiles, who was in ill health. Bill DeWitt Jr., an oil investor from Cincinnati, Ohio, told Bush about it. He also told him that Peter Ueberroth, the baseball commissioner, wanted someone with local connections to buy the team. Ueberroth felt that baseball in general was going through a bad time, what with charges of drug use in some instances and skyrocketing salaries and ticket prices. He did not want to make it worse by having outsiders coming in to take over the team. Bush was interested. In fact, he had long ago wanted to own a baseball team and had once dreamed of buying the Houston Astros.

After the election, Bush helped to put together a group of investors to purchase the Rangers. Ueberroth was not satisfied because he thought Bush's investors did not have enough local ties. So, Fort Worth financier Richard Rainwater was brought in. Bush used his own Harken stock as his investment along with some of his own money, which totaled about six hundred thousand dollars—the smallest investment of the group.

In April 1989 the group purchased the Texas Rangers and Bush, along with businessman Edward Rose, was named to run the team. Bush took on the public relations role for the team, and Rose handled the daily business activities.

As a baseball team, the Texas Rangers were a mess. They played in a dilapidated stadium built for minor league competition, and they were generally losers, even though they had one of baseball's best pitchers, superstar Nolan Ryan. Over the next two years, Bush worked hard to improve both the image and the team. Once again, he was everywhere, greeting the ballplayers, who grew to love him, walking around the ballpark during the games, and eating hot dogs with Laura in their seats next to the dugout. Once he showed up in the broadcast booth and delivered a short commentary in Spanish when Juan Gonzalez got a hit to break up a no-hitter. (The Ranger games are broadcast in Spanish as well as English.)

Bush even invited his mother to the ballpark that first year and, clad in a Rangers jacket, she threw out a ball to begin the game. He was not so happy with his mother, however, when soon after that, an article on him appeared in *Texas Monthly*. It speculated about his possible run for the governorship. When asked by the press about such a happening, his mother commented that he should

In 1989 Bush purchased the Texas Rangers baseball team. As head of the Rangers' public relations, Bush improved the team's image and won favorable publicity for himself.

concentrate on baseball. This angered the son a good deal, and in an interview, he said that his mother had been giving him advice for forty-two years, "most of which I haven't taken." Since that sounded a bit harsh, he added, "I love my mother, and appreciate her advice, but that's all it is, advice."[24] Nonetheless, that August, he said he would be staying on with the Rangers.

Bush's greatest contribution to the Rangers was his work to get a referendum passed for a new and much-needed stadium at a time when voters elsewhere were turning down similar high-priced projects. He became an avid booster for the stadium, using his influence to get corporations and individuals to pledge financial support. He went out of his way to woo critics of the project, such as Jim Reeves of the Fort Worth *Star-Telegram*. Bush convinced Reeves of the project's worth and eventually persuaded him to change his mind. Through interviews and speeches at local organizations, Bush tried to improve the team's image, always pointing out the talent of Nolan Ryan and the bright future that was ahead for the team as a whole. He proved to be an excellent salesman. In all, Bush received much favorable publicity from his association with the Texas Rangers.

However, Bush had also incurred a huge debt buying the Rangers, so in 1990, he sold two-thirds of his Harken shares to repay loans he had incurred. Iraq invaded Kuwait six weeks later, causing Harken's shares, as well as those of all American oil companies, to nosedive. Some speculated

Go Rangers!

In 1988, at the time Bush became one of the investors who bought the Texas Rangers baseball team, fans had little to celebrate. Part of the Western Division of the American League, the team arrived in the Dallas–Fort Worth area in 1972. Its scheduled first game on April 6 was cancelled by a players' strike. On April 21 when the season finally began, about twenty thousand fans sat in the thirty-five-thousand-plus-seat stadium, and that would be the second-largest crowd all season. The team's record was 54-100, but it was even worse in 1973 when the Rangers suffered through a win-loss total of 57-105.

In 1974 the team was sold to Bradford G. Corbett, a plastics tycoon, and its record improved to 84-76. Although the Rangers notched respectable records over the next few years, the team never finished higher than seventh in its league. With the arrival of superstar pitcher Nolan Ryan in 1989, things looked up. After Bush and his group bought the team, fan attendance increased. With a lease for twenty-two years, the franchise opened its new Ballpark in Arlington in 1994, when it finished first. In 1996, 1998, and 1999, the Rangers reached the playoffs but lost to the New York Yankees each time. In 2001 the team dazzled baseball fans when it bought the contract of shortstop Alex Rodriguez, considered perhaps the game's best player, for $252 million, covering a ten-year period. It was baseball's biggest deal ever. Now Ranger fans wait to see if it brings them the World Series trophy.

that Bush had advance knowledge of the coming invasion, which he denied. Harken also beat out many other U.S. companies to win a contract from Bahrain to drill offshore wells in the Persian Gulf. Some thought Harken might have gotten inside knowledge through Bush about that deal, too. Bush again denied any involvement.

All in all, Bush's decision to stay with baseball proved to be the right one for him. He gained popularity from his association with the national pastime. Said former fraternity brother Roland Betts:

Before the Rangers, I told him [Bush] he needed to do something to step out of his father's shadow. Baseball was it. He became our local celebrity. He knew every usher. He signed autographs. He talked to fans. His presence meant everything. His eyes were on politics the whole time, but even when he was speaking at Republican luncheons, he was always talking about the Rangers.[25]

For a man with his eye on the governor's seat, it was a great political move.

Chapter 4
In the Governor's Seat

When President George H. W. Bush lost his reelection bid to William Jefferson Clinton in 1992, he dropped from the national spotlight, and the younger Bush took his first major step toward building his own political career. Once again, the son had campaigned diligently for his father, but this time it was no use. The American public wanted a change, and the Democratic candidates were elected.

An Eye on 1994

Bush set a formidable task for himself when he decided to run for governor of Texas in 1994. In fact, some of his friends thought he was joking. They urged him to wait another four years. The reason for all the consternation was the current governor, Ann Richards. She talked tough, she rode motorcycles, and Texans loved her even before she had beaten oilman Clayton Williams for the governor's spot in 1990. Her most famous line to the press, which made her the darling of the Democrats, was uttered at the Democratic convention in 1988 when she said of Bush's father, "Poor George, he was born with a silver foot in his mouth."[26]

Born and educated in Texas, Richards had been state treasurer, becoming the first woman entering statewide office in Texas in fifty years. As governor, she focused on education programs and stressed government efficiency. She was an awesome, no-nonsense force who spent most of her waking moments extolling the state of Texas. She loved doing it, and she attracted voters by the droves. She was certainly a unique character, even for the brash politics of Texas. But Bush thought he could beat her.

The Campaign

When Bush hit the campaign trail to unseat Richards, he made the decision to run on his own, never mentioning his father nor asking him to make appearances. Bush proved to be an effective campaigner, more articulate and a better debater than his father. And he was not timid about matching wisecracks with the governor, already known for her legendary off-the-cuff remarks.

Bush first had to define the issues that were important to the minds of the 18 million Texas voters. He knew that crime was a hot issue, and he asserted that crime had risen 6 percent since Richards had taken office. He promised a war on sex offenders and rapists, stating that they would not be given parole under any circumstances, even though in reality the Texas governor has little or no power to influence early release. The other big issues were welfare reform and education. Bush proposed that bounty hunters be sent after fathers who reneged on their child support payments. His welfare plan also aimed at ending payments for a family after two years. Richards countered that such an act was punishing newborn children, but Bush felt that her response would not go over well with the Texas voters, who were already smarting over rising welfare costs. On education, Bush opposed a property tax which shifted money from the wealthier areas into poorer ones.

The Bush team concentrated on portraying their candidate as a man of change. The strategy was to harp on what made people discontented—rising crime, poor education, expanding welfare rolls—and to say little about what people disliked, such as taxes. And Bush was to keep quiet when hit with a personal attack.

Bush got the message and stuck to the strategy. He campaigned on education and welfare reform and reducing crime, but he rarely got into specifics about what he would do in each case. What he did do was refuse to answer the many challenges from Richards about his lack of experience, his overindulgence in alcohol, and his ties to the eastern establishment. Perhaps the deepest attacks from Richards pointed out his zero success as a political leader. Her campaign team said he hid his inexperience behind a great show of self-confidence—and behind his name.

But in the end, it was more the personalities than the issues that won the race. Richards so severely berated her opponent that voters began to think she was being too harsh and unfair. Some say the sharp tongue that had gotten her into the governor's mansion now helped to get her out.

Whatever the reasons, Bush won his first race for governor by a margin of 54 to 46 percent. His father called from Houston to offer his proud congratulations. It was a most important milestone in Bush's political career. He was finally on his own.

Running the State

The Bush family, including thirteen-year-old twins Jenna and Barbara, moved into the governor's mansion in Austin, and Bush put his shares in the Texas Rangers into a blind trust. (A blind trust means that the owner does not know what is happening to his or her stocks and bonds while in office. The trust is administered by someone else.) He also moved his mostly autographed 250 baseballs into his new office. Now it was time to govern the state.

Bush was a whirlwind again, arriving at the office at 8:00 A.M., jogging in the late morning, and allowing work to last no longer than 9:00 P.M. so he could spend time with his family. Staff meetings were

In 1994 Bush ran for governor of Texas against incumbent Ann Richards, known for her tough character. Despite her popularity, Bush won the election by a narrow margin.

brief, and everybody was urged to give an opinion. During his first term, he concentrated on education and business reform, but some charged that he spent too much time on what they called his pet projects and ignored environmental concerns and unemployment.

To gain more money for education in the state, Bush proposed changing the way education was funded. Vowing to change the method of having wealthier communities pay higher property taxes to provide education money to the poor communities, he proposed cutting property taxes by $3 billion and increasing the state sales tax. The proposal went down to a stinging defeat, and the legislature found its own way to cut property taxes. However, Bush's Texas Reading Initiative program, aimed at reading proficiency by the third grade, did improve statewide educational testing results. With these and similar programs, he seemed genuinely determined to improve the lives of the poor.

THE BUSH PHILOSOPHY

The new governor wasted no time in making his philosophy of government known to the people of Texas: he is a conservative Republican. In general, a conservative is one who believes in the traditions and institutions that have proven themselves over time. A conservative believes in keeping the present political, social, and economic order as much as possible. Conservatives, in political terms, are said to be to the right of center. In contrast, a liberal is said to be to the left. In general, liberals believe that the main function of the government is to protect the rights of citizens and are usually characterized as reformers—enemies of old traditions and customs.

Bush also calls himself a compassionate conservative, which skeptics say means a Republican seeking Democratic votes. Compassionate conservatism says it is compassionate to help people in need, but such help must be accounted for financially and must show results. Bush is against big government, believing that government should do only a few things for the people but do them well. Government spending for Bush is not compassionate. People must be encouraged to build lives on their own.

The new governor made it clear at the beginning of his first term that he believed in tradition and social stability. In his speeches, he stressed the importance of established institutions such as the church, the family, and class structure. He spoke of gradual rather than abrupt political change. For Bush, the government should have only a limited role in people's lives, which is why he was against the Texas welfare system as it stood.

The new governor concentrated on welfare reform and decreased the welfare rolls by one-half during his first term. Some of that decrease, however, was attributed to a thriving national economy that increased employment. Bush also encouraged local and church communities to take over some of the welfare duties, thereby relieving the state's burden. On the abortion issue, he opposed it but would not fight to overturn *Roe v.*

After winning the race for governor, Bush moved into the governor's mansion in Austin with his wife and twin daughters Barbara and Jenna.

Wade, the landmark Supreme Court decision allowing legal abortion.

On abortion and related issues, Bush did not satisfy the so-called Christian conservatives. They had supported his election, although most of these voters were to the right of Bush's politics. He actually came to a crisis with them over an event in January 1998, near the end of his first term. Despite his campaign rhetoric about prisoners and paroles, Bush had pretty much left the prison system alone during his first term. Now, Karla Faye Tucker, sentenced for a pickax murder, was sitting on death row about to become the first white woman executed in Texas since the Civil War. Tucker claimed she had undergone a spiritual conversion in prison and was a born-again Christian. Members of the Christian Right, including well-known evangelist Pat Robertson, asked that Tucker's life be spared. Although Bush was reminded of the strength of the Christian Right in Texas, he refused to intervene. He said he had to let the prison board do its job.

Running for his second term as governor in the fall of 1998 against Democrat Garry Mauro, Bush ran on the issue of changing the state's tax code, which he thought would sit well with the voters in a presidential election. As the campaign got into full gear, the economy of Texas, the eleventh largest in the world, was humming along, since Texas businesses were now more focused on computer software and airlines than on the unpredictable markets of gas and oil. Because of the economic climate, Bush promised higher state taxes on business instead of the local property taxes to help fund public schools. This was the big issue that he felt would assure his reelection.

Bush was also faced with many deep problems in Texas such as the overflow of illegal immigrants and their extreme poverty. How to help them without a revolt from the white majority was an ever-present issue. For Bush, always short on details in his campaign rhetoric, his broad answer was "a responsible society built on tough individualism and Bible-belt solidity."[27]

Bush's campaign strategy worked. His winning margin in his bid for reelection was big: he garnered about half of the

VIOLENCE JUST BELOW THE SURFACE

If Bush annoyed the conservative right with his refusal to stay the execution of Karla Faye Tucker in early 1998, a few months later, he did the right thing as far as conservatives were concerned by his refusal to get involved in the murder of James Byrd Jr., a forty-nine-year-old African American of Jasper, Texas. Byrd was beaten unconscious in June of that year, chained to the back of a pickup truck, and dragged over rural roads until he died. The three men accused of his murder all had ties to white supremacist groups. This rural part of east Texas is one of the poorest and least educated in the nation, with barely half the adult population graduating from high school. Racial hatred has long been a problem there.

Bush condemned the brutal murder, but he refused to travel to Jasper personally to show that he was outraged over the atrocity. Critics charged that he did not want to get involved in any friction between blacks and whites in the area.

Hispanic vote and 67 percent overall. He was the only governor in Texas history to win two four-year terms in a row.

THE MAN BEHIND THE SMILE

Even after four years in office and beginning a second term, Bush's friends said he had not changed all that much: if he could, he would still work in an office that reached the stage of near-anarchy. His jacket was more often than not thrown on the floor, and papers were strewn all over the place. That problem was solved in the governor's office by setting up two rooms. Bush with his jacket on greeted guests in a neat and tidy outer room, and the inner office was left to himself and his satisfying clutter.

As governor, Bush continued to care little about clothes and has never in his life been described as a snappy dresser. In fact, he once easily won the Midland Country Club's prize for the worst-dressed golfer. Although he prefers old sports shirts and jeans, as governor he did buy a number of dark suits all at once so that he had something a little less shabby to wear when he was out shaking hands with voters. His reelection team implied that this disregard for clothes showed the down-to-earth quality of the man.

During his crowded days in the governor's office, Bush still found time for a jog or workout. As usual, it was difficult for him to sit still, which is one of the reasons he is not known as much of a reader. He was always punctual for meetings, and he insisted that they start on time, a trait that is somewhat novel in political circles. Bush's easy going, friendly demeanor was a great asset and often hid the fact that he has a sharp tongue, which he says he inherits from his mother. He was noted for teasing his office staff with nicknames for them. He seemed unabashed by whoever was in his presence, a trait that sometimes worried his aides because they were afraid that his sarcasm, even if kindly meant, might cause hurt feelings or worse.

In all, Bush made quite a remarkable transformation from his first halting foray into politics as a champion of the oil industry to a governor who wanted to make sure that children learned to read and that poor people got jobs. From the brash young hotshot who drank too much, he was now the still brash-talking but quieter man who was past the half-century mark, still tenuous perhaps in his leadership but secure in his religion and himself. And this politician of new image now had his eye on a new address—in Washington, D.C.

A NEW CAMPAIGN

The first step on Bush's journey from Midland to the White House began to take shape from the governor's mansion in Texas. Bush had thought about running for the presidency as far back as the summer of 1997 when he learned he was first choice among those who would decide on a candidate for the Republican nomination in 2000. Not lost on the

As governor of Texas, Bush was known for his casual attire and easygoing demeanor. Bush's aides exploited his down-to-earth qualities during his bid for the presidency.

pollsters was the perhaps frivolous but intriguing fact that if Bush ran and won, he would be the first son of a president to reach the White House since John Quincy Adams in 1825.

The decision to run was made soon after Bush was inaugurated for his second term in Austin. But he claims there was no "magic moment" when it happened. He says he talked over the prospect with his wife and daughters that Christmas. Although Laura and the twins, as well as the extended Bush family, have always loyally supported his ambitions, it is no secret that the teenaged twins were less than thrilled at the prospect of moving to Washington, D.C., and being trailed by the Secret Service twenty-four hours a day. In fact, Bush later admitted to being somewhat dismayed by how little the girls joined the campaign trail, which was practically not at all, after he announced his candidacy.

GETTING THE NOMINATION

Once Bush decided to run for the White House in 2000, he put his team into place. They were the same advisers who had

Bush takes the oath of office for his second term as governor, becoming the only governor in Texas history to win two consecutive four-year terms.

guided him to victory as governor—Karl Rove, Joseph Allbaugh, and Karen Hughes. Rove was the chief strategist, Allbaugh the campaign manager, and Hughes was Bush's communications director and confidant on campaign issues. Their strategy, like that of other candidates, was to win as many early state primary elections as possible. Primary elections are held to determine who will be the candidates to run for office. All U.S. states use some form of direct primary, meaning that the voters choose the party candidates for office.

In order to enter a state's primary, the candidate either declares that he or she is in the running, is chosen at a preprimary convention, or (the most common method) gets a required number of voters to sign a nomination petition. The earliest of the primaries for a national election are generally held in February before the election in November. The winner of the first two or three primaries, depending upon the margin of victory and other factors, is generally regarded as the favorite to be chosen formally later in the year at the party's national convention.

Campaigning in the primaries, Bush had to keep those who had backed him in the governor's race but also try to rein in new voters. He felt fairly confident about keeping his conservative voters with his views on national defense and moral values. He also tried to reach a wider audience by being "compassionate" about such things as improving low-performance schools. This time, his name was of immediate great help because everyone knew it. If they did not know him, they certainly knew his father as president for four years. (In fact, there was a rumor that some people actually thought his father was running again.) Bush's campaign speeches often included mention of or stories about various members of his family, including his wife and his mother. His friendly personality also aided him immensely, as did his reelection as governor, which showed he was a winner. However, he faced hard questions about serving in the National Guard instead of going to Vietnam, about rumors of past drug use, which he has always denied, and his vast inexperience in national politics. His critics were also severe in their condemnation of his nonexistent environmental policies. Others questioned whether he was intelligent enough to function in the position of president.

Such accusations began to damage Bush's early lead, and at the presidential primary in New Hampshire in February 2000, Senator John McCain was the winner. A week later, Bush won in South Carolina, but McCain won again later that month in Michigan. In response to the losses, the Bush team adopted a new strategy. The man from Texas would campaign as the man of the people. He would use his own lack of political experience to his advantage. In fact, his inexperience was to be viewed as setting him free from the trappings and ties of bureaucratic Washington, D.C. Such a candidate, said the campaign team, was just what the country needed to restore decency, honor, and family values to a government that sorely needed them.

As the primary season continued, the new strategy seemed to be working, and

> ### PRESIDENT MOM
>
> Bush says he grew up with the laser stares of his mother and still experiences them once in a while today. The former first lady is known for expressing her opinions and getting her way—at least within the family. She is "tough," according to her oldest son. He remembers that he and his siblings never wanted to get up to go to church on Sundays. However, he says, they went. He also says that she was always there to take the kids to Cub Scout meetings and ball games.
>
> Bush says that he and his mother have developed a kind of joking back-and-forth relationship that has been going on for years. His mother is more blunt. She says they fight all the time but hastily adds the reason is that mother and son are so alike.

Bush began to roll up a good lead over McCain, who proved the only serious challenger to the Bush nomination. When the Republican National Convention opened in Philadelphia on Monday, July 31, 2000, everyone knew that the voting on Thursday night would be only a formality. Bush went to the convention with 62 percent of the delegate's votes to 32 percent for McCain and far lesser figures for the others still technically in the race. When the roll call was taken on August 4, Bush received a nearly unanimous vote as the Republican candidate for president of the United States.

Chapter 5
The Disputed Election

The 2000 campaign began for Bush at the Republican National Convention on August 4 in a spirit of party harmony and propelled him into perhaps the most polarizing national election in the country's history. In his fifty-one-minute acceptance speech to the delegation, Bush promised to renew America's purpose—to seize what he called a moment of American promise. He promised to save social security, to put payroll taxes into sound, responsible investments, and to reform the tax code. Concerning the military, he said that "When America uses force in the world, the cause must be just, the goal must be clear, and the victory must be overwhelming."[28] Bush again called himself a compassionate conservative as well as "the best leader for changing times," saying that the Republicans had become "the party of ideas and innovation, the party of idealism and inclusion."[29]

To the surprise of many, Bush selected Richard (Dick) Cheney as his running mate. Cheney had been the elder Bush's secretary of defense, but he had been involved in big business in recent years and was not well known to the general public. Experts say Cheney was not Bush's first choice for the job. He had wanted Colin Powell, the well-liked former chairman of the Joint Chiefs of Staff who guided the successful operation of the Gulf War in 1990–1991 when the elder Bush was in office. But Powell did not want the position. Bush's second choice was Florida senator Connie Mack, who was also not interested.

THE RUN FOR THE BIG PRIZE

The Republican ticket of Bush and Cheney faced a formidable challenge by Democrats Al Gore and Joseph Lieberman. It seemed that Gore's political experience alone, to say nothing of Lieberman's, would make them a shoo-in.

Al (for Albert) Gore Jr. was a Washington, D.C., native and had just spent the last eight years as vice president of the United States during the administration of Bill Clinton. Before that, he had spent eight years in the House and four years as a U.S. senator from Tennessee. Harvard educated, he was a leader on environmental issues and had published a book called *Earth in the Balance: Ecology and the Human Spirit*, describing the problems that threaten the survival of the earth. Yale-educated Joseph

Bush announces at a press conference that he has agreed to participate in five nationally televised debates against Democratic presidential candidate Al Gore.

Lieberman had served as a U.S. senator from Connecticut since 1989.

There was no way that Bush and Cheney could challenge the experience of the Gore-Lieberman ticket, so Bush's team wisely did not. Instead, they largely ignored that issue, concentrating instead on Gore's closeness to President Bill Clinton. And the strategy worked. The reason was not Gore but the outgoing president.

Bill Clinton served eight years as a liberal and generally popular president. Born poor in Arkansas, he was highly intelligent and likeable. He won a Rhodes scholarshp to Oxford University and graduated from Yale Law School where he met and later married fellow law student Hillary Rodham. In 1992, he challenged and defeated George H. W. Bush with 43 percent of the vote and an electoral college landslide. In 1996, he became the first Democratic president since Franklin D. Roosevelt to be elected to office twice, winning by a good margin over Republican Robert Dole.

One of Clinton's great successes was balancing the federal budget; when the 1998 fiscal year ended, there was a surplus of $70 billion, the first surplus in a generation. But Clinton had personal troubles in the final years of his administration. The major problem was charges of perjury, obstruction of justice, and abuse of power that stemmed from his extramarital relationship with White House intern Monica Lewinsky. Clinton at first denied involvement, but eventually admitted what he had done. Because he had denied the accusations under oath, he was subject to the charge of perjury. The House Judiciary Committee began impeachment hearings in late 1998.

In December, Clinton became the first elected U.S. president to be impeached. (Andrew Johnson was impeached in 1868, but he had entered office not through election but because of the assassination of Abraham Lincoln.) When the impeachment failed to remove him from office, Clinton served out the rest of his term battling the Republican majority in Congress over a number of issues.

Because much of the country was either disgusted or at least embarrassed by Clinton's misbehavior, Bush used every opportunity in his campaign speeches to link Gore with the former president, even though Gore had a reputation for moral correctness as strong as any of Bush's rhetoric. Bush constantly referred to the "Clinton-Gore team," rarely ever speaking of Gore's record as vice president or as a lawmaker. "For eight years," said Bush, "the Clinton-Gore administration has coasted through prosperity. And the path of least resistance is always downhill. . . . Not this time, not this year," he continued. "This is not the time for new changes, this is the time for new beginnings."[30]

THE MONEY BACKERS

Also helping Bush in his bid for the presidency were many powerful American business people; business interests in America have long favored Republican candidates over Democrats. An example of how helpful big business can be is what the Bush team called the "Pioneers," about 150 powerful businesspeople who, by bundling contributions from individuals,

Bush initially chose Colin Powell (left), the former chairman of the Joint Chiefs of Staff, as his running mate. However, he eventually settled on Dick Cheney (right), his father's secretary of defense.

each raised about one hundred thousand dollars to support him. Individual contributions by law cannot exceed one thousand dollars each.

Bush was so successful as a fundraiser that he took in some $67 million through 1999, four times more than Gore, McCain, and Senator Bill Bradley of New Jersey (the latter having challenged Gore for the Democratic nomination) combined. In a practical sense, that meant that if Democratic funds dwindled during the campaign, they might, for instance, have to limit the number of expensive—but effective—television ads for their candidate, whereas Bush would not be limited in that way.

THE STRANGEST ELECTION NIGHT IN HISTORY

The campaign of 2000 was gritty, grinding, and not much on statesmanlike speeches. Bush was generally short on details for his proposed policies. And for all his experience and background, Gore proved to be a rather ponderous and ineffective speaker, sometimes overshadowed by his less experienced but self-confident opponent. In what seemed an obvious move to distance himself from Bill Clinton and perhaps Bush's insinuations, Gore did not call on the still-popular president to campaign for him or even to speak for him on occasion. Many pundits later called that a major campaign mistake.

And so, on election night, November 7, 2000, the race was very close. As the night wore on and states went to one candidate or the other with the electoral vote essentially split down the middle, it became clear that Florida was the key state. Whoever took Florida with its twenty-five electoral votes would probably win.

At about 6:50 P.M. central daylight time in Austin, Texas, Bush, family members, and friends had gathered in the Shoreline Grill. Jeb Bush, governor of Florida, seemed most nervous. It was joked that he would be the black sheep of the family if he could not deliver his state to his brother. Then the news broke; the network projected Gore as the winner in Florida. Everyone was devastated. Bush's twin daughters cried and were hugged by their father.

Soon, however, the media was not so sure. And then, at 1:16 A.M., central daylight time, Fox TV News declared Bush the winner in Florida. A short time later, all the networks chalked Florida up for Bush.

Bush attacked his opponent Al Gore by linking him with outgoing president Bill Clinton, who had been impeached for lying about his affair with a White House intern.

THE DISPUTED ELECTION ■ 63

Gore, who was drafting a victory speech, could not believe it.

As the day wore on, though, Bush's lead kept shrinking. With 98 percent of the vote in, Bush had a lead of fifty thousand votes. Then it fell to only five hundred votes with 99.5 percent of the vote counted. Gore, who had called Bush earlier to concede (his aides had warned him not to), now called back to say the race was too close to call.

The telephone conversation between the two men was undoubtedly not amusing to them that night, but read years later it has amusing overtones. As recorded in *Newsweek*:

> "Circumstances have changed dramatically since I first called you," Gore began. "The state of Florida is too close to call."
>
> Bush was brusque and a little incredulous. "Are you saying what I think you're saying?" he demanded. "Let me make sure that I understand. You're calling back to retract that concession?"
>
> "Don't get snippy about it!" Gore said, as his listening aides tried not to laugh. "Let me explain," Gore went on. If Bush won the recount, Gore would support him. But it was too soon to be claiming Florida.
>
> Bush begged to differ. His brother, the governor of Florida, was standing right there, and he was reporting a Bush victory in the state.
>
> Gore coolly said something to the effect that Bush's brother was not the final arbiter of victory in Florida.
>
> Now it was Bush's turn to be cold. "Do what you have to do," he said, and hung up.[31]

Bush and Gore were not the only ones to be frustrated. The television networks were in a frenzy of embarrassment and indecision. Now they reclaimed Florida from the Bush camp and announced that the state was still too close to call. Moaned anchorman Tom Brokaw of NBC, "We don't have egg on our face. We have an omelet." It was said that the executive editor of the *New York Times* actually had to deliver those famous three words, "Stop the presses!"[32] The *Times* had reportedly already run off 115,000 copies declaring Bush the winner.

As time wore on, the whole picture grew more complicated, because it was becoming apparent that Gore was going to win the popular vote nationwide. Reports of voting irregularities in Florida began to come in. Some voters in Palm Beach County said their votes were thrown out because the ballot was confusing and they had inadvertently voted twice. The ballot had been printed in large type for elderly voters with punch holes beside the candidates' names. But the layout of the ballot did not make it clear which punch hole belonged to which candidate. Some voters did not know which one to punch, sometimes punching holes on either

Bush laughs with his brother Jeb Bush, governor of Florida, after reports confirm his victory in the 2000 election. Voting irregularities in Florida, however, forced a recount, and the results were not finalized until days later.

side of the candidate's name and, therefore, voting twice, which made the ballot invalid. An indication of the faulty positioning of the punch holes was the fact that right-wing, ultraconservative candidate Pat Buchanan got more than three thousand votes in an area with a strong aging Jewish liberal population. There was certain to be a recount.

There were problems in other counties too, and it began to look as though the presidency of the United States was going to be decided by something with the unlikely name of a "hanging chad." On the outdated punch-card ballots that were used in Florida, the voter had to punch the hole open to vote. If a piece of paper (a hanging chad) remained in the hole, as often apparently happened, the vote was not counted. So in several Florida counties, a manual recount was ordered.

THE COURTS STEP IN

The election of 2000 was not decided on election night, nor the next morning, as sometimes has happened, nor even the next day. On Sunday, November 12, the recount began, ordered by Florida secretary of state Katherine Harris, to be completed by 5:00 P.M. Tuesday, November 14, while the country—and the candidates—waited. On Tuesday, the Bush team entered a legal challenge to stop the manual recounts. The challenge was rejected.

When some counties requested more time to count the ballots, the case went to the Florida Supreme Court, which ruled that the recount should go on but only until 5:00 P.M. on November 26. Even though some recounts had still not been concluded by then, Harris declared that Bush had won Florida, giving him the state's twenty-five electoral votes and

DOUBLE TROUBLE

Just as Bush was getting settled in the White House in mid-2001, his twin daughters, Jenna and Barbara, who were nineteen at the time, got into trouble with the law. Barbara, described as the more studious and quiet twin and studying at Yale University, was charged with using a fake ID card at a local bar. The week before, Jenna, a University of Texas student, had been charged the second time with using a borrowed ID card in an Austin, Texas, restaurant. Both girls were cited by authorities for underage drinking.

The president let the twins know he was not happy and asked them to Camp David the next weekend for a talk. Media experts say that even though they were probably not anxious to see their father, they were probably more reluctant to meet their grandmother, Barbara Bush, who was also at Camp David that weekend. She is known in family circles as "the enforcer."

putting him over the top in the electoral vote count. But the true vote count in Florida was never tallied. Gore immediately challenged the Florida Supreme Court, claiming he would be the winner if all the votes were counted. Now the Florida legislature stepped in. It said it had the power to select electors to the electoral college, and so it chose Bush as the winner. But Gore and Bush still battled over the vote count in some counties.

More than a month after the bizarre election, Bush's lawyers took the case to the U.S. Supreme Court, arguing that the hand recounts in some counties violated the equal protection of the law for voters in those counties that were not being recounted. On December 9, the Court stopped the recounts temporarily. On December 12, by a vote of seven to two, the Court sent the case back to the Florida court. But the Court did not extend the deadline for counting the ballots. There was literally no time left to complete the count. George Bush won the state of Florida, but because of the confusing ballots, legal fighting, hanging chads, obvious discrepancies in voting procedures, and political chaos, many felt he had not truly been elected president, especially in light of the fact that he had lost the popular vote. Some called him the accidental president. It was an inauspicious way to begin an administration, and Bush well realized that it would take some time for the wounds to heal.

"I hope I'll never have to go through another evening like I did," Jeb Bush said after it was all over. "It was one of the most amazing and emotionally intense evenings of my life."[33] He felt that he was at fault for not being able to deliver the state of Florida to his brother. He apologized to Bush when the news first came in that Gore had taken the state. But with Bush's victory, critics claimed that Jeb had pulled strings in Florida to get his brother elected. He dismissed such charges by saying, "Vote fraud in our state is a felony. We will prosecute it to the fullest extent of the law."[34]

UNTIL THE TERRORISTS CAME

All the bitterness and doubt that followed the election of 2000 left Bush in a tenuous position as the forty-third president of the United States. Few really knew him, whether they were politicians in Washington or voters in the rest of the country.

He was inaugurated in January 2001, and immediately after the ceremony, the public got its first images of the new personalities in the White House. That evening, Bush and his wife attended the obligatory inaugural balls, as all presidents do. But it was obvious that even on the dance floor, the new president was going to stick to a tight schedule as he had done as governor. The Bushes did go to all nine inaugural balls, but spent a combined total of seven minutes and five seconds on the dance floor. They were back at their new home in the White House before midnight, well ahead of the schedule that had been outlined.

The President's Right Hand

Since becoming assistant to the president for national security affairs, generally referred to as the national security adviser, Condoleezza Rica has become Bush's closest and most trusted aide. Born in Birmingham, Alabama, in 1954, Rice studied at the University of Denver, earned a master's degree from Notre Dame in 1975, and received a PhD from Denver in 1981. Soon after, she joined the faculty of Stanford University in Palo Alto, California, where she spent six years as the university's provost—the chief budget and academic officer. She was responsible for a $1.5 billion annual budget and was in charge of some fourteen thousand students and fourteen hundred staff.

Rice also served in the elder Bush's administration as director and senior director of Soviet and East European affairs in the National Security Council. In addition, she was special assistant to the director of the Joint Chiefs of Staff in 1986. Rice has been on the board of numerous corporations and has earned a number of honorary doctorate degrees.

Bush now began to gather around him the people who would be important in his administration. He continued his style of governing, carrying out an on-schedule routine as much as possible. Laura Bush played much the same role as in the governor's mansion, providing strong reassurance for her husband but staying out of the spotlight. Bush installed forceful people in his cabinet who would plan initiatives and carry them out. Besides Cheney, there was Secretary of State Colin Powell, Defense Secretary Donald Rumsfeld, and National Security Adviser Condoleezza Rice. Rumsfeld had a good deal of big-business experience and was the secretary of defense in the Gerald Ford administration. Rice became Bush's closest and most trusted adviser: she had served in the National Security Council during his father's term in office. In addition to his cabinet, Bush surrounded himself with a group who had worked with him in Texas for many years: he believes in team leadership.

Although Bush holds the office of president in highest respect, his demeanor is one of lightness around the halls of government. His attitude keeps his aides on their toes, especially as they must watch out for his penchant for misprounouncing words or the names of visiting foreign dignitaries. If such gaffes were noticed by the new president, he merely made fun of himself. All in all, he seemed confident in his new position, and the first months of his new administration were low-key, filled with getting a transition government running smoothly. He also spent a good deal of time trying to charm his Democratic opposition in Congress. Then he tried to mobilize the narrow Republican majority to propose a $1.6 million tax cut. When he found out he would have to compromise on that, he declared victory by settling for a smaller cut.

In the area of public communication, the new president did not receive high marks from most observers. His addresses to the public were few to begin with, and he seemed unprepared and unpolished during them. He met on only few occasions with the press. He appeared unaware of his role as the symbolic as well as actual leader of the country. For instance, he said nothing to the nation after racial disturbances rocked the city of Cincinnati, Ohio.

During this period, the American public was still making up its mind what it thought about the strange election just past and about the new occupant of the White House. Then the events of September 11, 2001, refocused everyone's attention—first on terrorism and then on George W. Bush.

Chapter 6
Policy at Home and Abroad

George W. Bush began his administration with a shaky mandate, but over the following months, he slowly and firmly sought to convince the public that his vision of America as leader of the free world was not only valid but righteous. He was able to succeed in large part because of the wave of patriotism that seized the United States after the terrible events of September 11, 2001. Even Bush's most severe critics dared not challenge him with the country caught up in a mood of fear, anger, and a desire for revenge.

NOT SINCE PEARL HARBOR

On September 11, 2001—for the first time since the bombing of Pearl Harbor in Hawaii in 1941, which brought the United States into World War II—America was attacked on its own soil. Two early morning flights from Boston were hijacked and deliberately crashed into the Twin Towers of the World Trade Center in New York City. A short time later, a third hijacked plane crashed into the Pentagon in the nation's capital, causing part of the building to collapse. A fourth hijacked plane crashed in Pennsylvania. By midmorning, both Trade Center towers had collapsed, killing thousands of workers, policemen, firefighters, and bystanders.

For a short time after the Twin Towers collapsed and the Pentagon building was in flames from terrorist attacks, the president of the United States was missing—or so it seemed to the American people. In fact, for most of the time directly following the tragedy, Bush was aloft in *Air Force One*.

THE IMMEDIATE AFTERMATH

Immediately after the second plane hit the second tower, the Secret Service insisted that the president take to the air. His top political aide, Karl Rove, told him there were credible threats to his safety. The Secret Service wanted to get *Air Force One* off the ground and into the protective cover of F-15 and F-16 fighter planes. Then they wanted to get Bush west, away from the chaos of the attacks on the East Coast. When Rove was later questioned about the decision, he replied, "You don't argue with the Secret Service."[35] However, for some time after the attacks, many people, both in government and out, had the impression that the Bush administration was not in charge or handling the crisis.

After landing at Barksdale Air Force Base in Louisiana, where *Air Force One* was refueled, the president broadcast a brief message to the American people. In this first attempt to assure a jittery and understandably frightened public, he sounded jittery himself. Bush said that the U.S. military had been put on high alert and that all possible security measures had been taken. Advised this time to fly into the interior of the country, he took off on *Air Force One* for the relative safety of Nebraska.

Those who were aboard at the time say it was a strange flight, as though the leader of the free world was on the run in

Air Force One

For a few hours after the terrorist attack of September 11, 2001, the president of the United States was up in *Air Force One,* which is often called the "flying White House." That is because while aloft in the plane, the president and staff have full access to nearly everything they would need on the ground. Information can be accessed quickly from the plane's communciations systems. The president can reach anyone he needs by secure telephones. Besides television and fax services, there are full printing, word processing, and photocopying services. Except for being able to walk out the door, the president and staff can continue their work as though they were on the ground. But strictly speaking, there is no one plane that is "Air Force One." Two specially built Boeing 747-200B series planes, Air Force designation VC-25A with tail numbers of 28000 and 29000, are available to the president. When the president is aboard either one, or aboard any other aircraft, the radio call sign is "Air Force One."

Until World War II, presidents did little traveling around the world because it was too time-consuming and the president would have been out of communication with the government for too long. In 1944, President Franklin D. Roosevelt created the Presidential Pilot Office to provide transportation for the chief executive. The first jet aircraft designated *Air Force One,* a Boeing 707, appeared in 1962.

Lyndon B. Johnson became president aboard *Air Force One* after the assassination of John F. Kennedy in 1963. When Richard Nixon resigned in 1974, *Air Force One* flew him home, but when the pilots received word in flight that Gerald Ford had been sworn in as president, the radio call sign was changed to SAM (for special air mission) 27000.

The Presidential Airlift Group takes care of these planes and is based at Andrews Air Force Base in Suitland, Maryland. The VC-25A, which seats more than seventy passengers, can fly halfway around the world before it needs to refuel.

Bush confers with New York mayor Rudy Giuliani and Governor George Pataki aboard Air Force One on September 11, 2001. Bush's aides insisted that he take to the air due to security concerns.

his own country. As Bush departed for Nebraska, other actions were taking place all over the nation. A state of emergency was declared in the capital. San Francisco International Airport was evacuated when it was learned that the city had been the destination of United Airlines Flight 93, which had crashed in Pennsylvania. Five warships and two aircraft carriers made preparations to get under way from Naval Station Norfolk in Norfolk, Virginia, to protect the eastern seaboard.

While Bush was aloft, he was not out of touch with the rest of the country's leadership. He was, in fact, in frequent contact with the vice president. Their most urgent concern was trying to decide if passenger planes coming into New York or Washington might be connected with what was obviously a terrorist plot. Reportedly, Bush ordered military pilots to shoot down any civilian plane, even loaded with passengers, if it refused commands to change direction away from either city. Shortly, all incoming civilian aircraft were diverted to Canada. During this period, Bush placed a call to his father, who had once had to make a decision about going to war. At this point, the administration thought more attacks were possible and that Bush might have to order the military to retaliate.

After being assured that safeguards long set in place to respond to a dangerous threat were quickly being enforced, and after Bush had spoken to the public, members of Congress started to grumble about the president's absence. They felt he had to get back to the Oval Office. As noted in *Newsweek*,

"People were angry and full of questions," said a senator who was there. Senators were especially angry when White House communications aide Karen Hughes emerged in Washington to assure the nation that the president was safe. "We didn't need her to tell us he was all right," said another senator. "We needed him to tell us that we are all right. They missed the point."[36]

Bush briefly broadcast from the White House that night. But his message was not inspiring, although he did promise revenge against the terrorist actions. After that, he seemed to reassure his staff by reassuring himself that he would stand strong in this most horrible of happenings. The crisis certainly demanded a level of leadership that he had neither witnessed nor exhibited before.

Bush rose to the challenge, particularly in the area of public communication. He sounded more assertive in his next few broadcasts. He was seen more frequently in public, presenting himself at both the World Trade Center and the Pentagon within a few days of the tragedies. *Time* magazine asked in an article headline: "Is the crisis changing Bush from a detached Chief Executive to an inspiring leader?"[37] On the morning after the disaster, presidential adviser Hughes arrived in the Oval Office to talk about photos that would be taken that day, but Bush had other ideas. "We need to tell the people that an act of war has been committed," he said. "This is a different kind of enemy than we have ever faced, and they need to know that."[38]

The War on Terror Begins

Bush apparently read the mood of the country well. Journalists would later comment that Americans had lost their innocence that day. The long-standing view that U.S. land was safe from foreign intruders was forever gone. Even when the Japanese had bombed Pearl Harbor in 1941, the United States was not yet a superpower, and to many, Hawaii seemed a world away. New York and Washington, D.C., were major cities. Moreover, thousands of Americans were dead in the rubble of the World Trade Center and the Pentagon. Two days after the attack, Congress authorized Bush "to use all necessary and appropriate force against those nations, organizations, or persons he determines planned, authorized, committed, or aided the terrorist attacks that occurred on September 11, 2001, or harbored such organizations or persons."[39] At this point, the actual perpetrators were not known, although the Saudi Arabian terrorist Osama bin Laden, thought to been involved in earlier attacks on Americans overseas, was suspected.

Over the next few days, Bush's speeches began to show more authority and determination as he took on the leadership role and provided the first glimpses of his philosophy and ways of dealing with threats to the nation. He spoke movingly at the Washington National Cathedral during a memorial service for the victims at the end of the week. But behind the words of reassurance and compassion was the beginnings of a plan. Said Bush to the audience in the cathedral:

> We are here in the middle hour of our grief. So many have suffered a loss, and today we express our nation's sorrow. We come before God to pray for the missing dead, and for those who love them. . . .
>
> To the children and parents and spouses and families and friends of the lost, we offer the sympathy of the nation. And I assure you, you are not alone. Just three days removed from these events, Americans do not yet have the distance of history. But our responsibility to history is already clear: to answer these attacks and rid the world of evil.[40]

In November, Bush addressed the UN (United Nations) General Assembly for the first time and was more specific about answering the attacks on American soil. He focused on a "campaign of terror" against the terrorists. He assured all the world's leaders gathered there that each nation had a stake in the cause and asked for a "comprehensive commitment" from all:

> As we meet, the terrorists are planning more murder—perhaps in my country, or perhaps in yours. They kill because they aspire to dominate. They seek to overthrow governments and destabilize entire regions. . . . This threat cannot be ignored. This threat cannot be appeased. Civilization, itself, the civilization we share, is threatened. History will record our response, and judge or justify every nation in this hall. . . . We in America . . . have already made adjustments in our laws and in our daily lives. We're taking new measures to investigate terror and to

MASTER TERRORIST

A hero to many young Arabs and number one on America's most wanted terrorist list is an immensely wealthy Saudi Arabian known as Osama bin Laden. Probably now in his forties, he was born to a Yemeni family in Saudi Arabia but left there to fight in Afghanistan when the Soviets invaded the country in 1979. He established the Maktab al-Khidimat (MAK), which brought in fighters from all over the world to expel the invaders.

Bin Laden went back to his family's construction business after the Soviets withdrew from Afghanistan, but his antigovernment activities got him ousted from the country. From there he went to Sudan but was expelled from there also when the United States put pressure on the Sudanese government. After his return to Afghanistan, bin Laden began to call for a so-called holy war against the United States and for the killing of Jews.

The United States charges bin Laden with international terrorism, including the World Trade Center bombing in 1993, the killing of nineteen U.S. soldiers in Saudi Arabia in 1996, the bombing of American embassies in Africa in 1998, and an attack on the USS *Cole* in 2000.

---

protect against threats. . . . The leaders of all nations must now carefully consider their responsibilities and their future.[41]

After the tragedy of September 11, Bush's approval ratings shot up among both Republicans and Democrats. For a time at least, the new president could count on both political parties and the American people to stand strongly behind him.

STALKING TERROR IN AFGHANISTAN

Within days of September 11, government officials had uncovered evidence that led them to believe that notorious terrorist Osama bin Laden was behind the attacks. The Saudi-born millionaire and intense militant was already well known to U.S. Secret Service operations. The United States charged that he had been responsible for the 1998 bombings of American embassies in Kenya and Tanzania. In late 1998, U.S. forces had destroyed what it said was a huge terrorist training compound run by bin Laden in Afghanistan. The action took place because the Afghanistan government, known as the Taliban, refused to turn over bin Laden. In the wake of the attacks on New York and Washington, Bush again called for Afghanistan to give bin Laden up.

Afghanistan is a landlocked, mostly desert land in south-central Asia. It has been a Muslim country since the seventh century, with various tribal dynasties heading the government since then. It was invaded by the Soviet Union in 1979. The Afghanistan war of 1979–1989 took an enormous toll on human and economic resources, and the Soviets withdrew. By early 1992, a guerrilla alliance set up a new government, but the alliance could not stay united. In late 1994, a group of Islamic students, the Taliban, took over the government, but it did not have control of most of the country.

Members of the Taliban operated under the leadership of Mohammad Omar to unite a divided nation under a fierce and fundamental strain of Islamic law. After the Taliban had initial successes fighting local warlords, its members captured the eastern city of Jalalabad, which borders Pakistan, and then occupied Kabul, the capital of Afghanistan, on September 27, 1996. As a result of years of fighting, the country was in a state of extensive destruction and chaos. People welcomed the Taliban with its promise to bring peace, and by June 1997, its militia was in general control of most of the land.

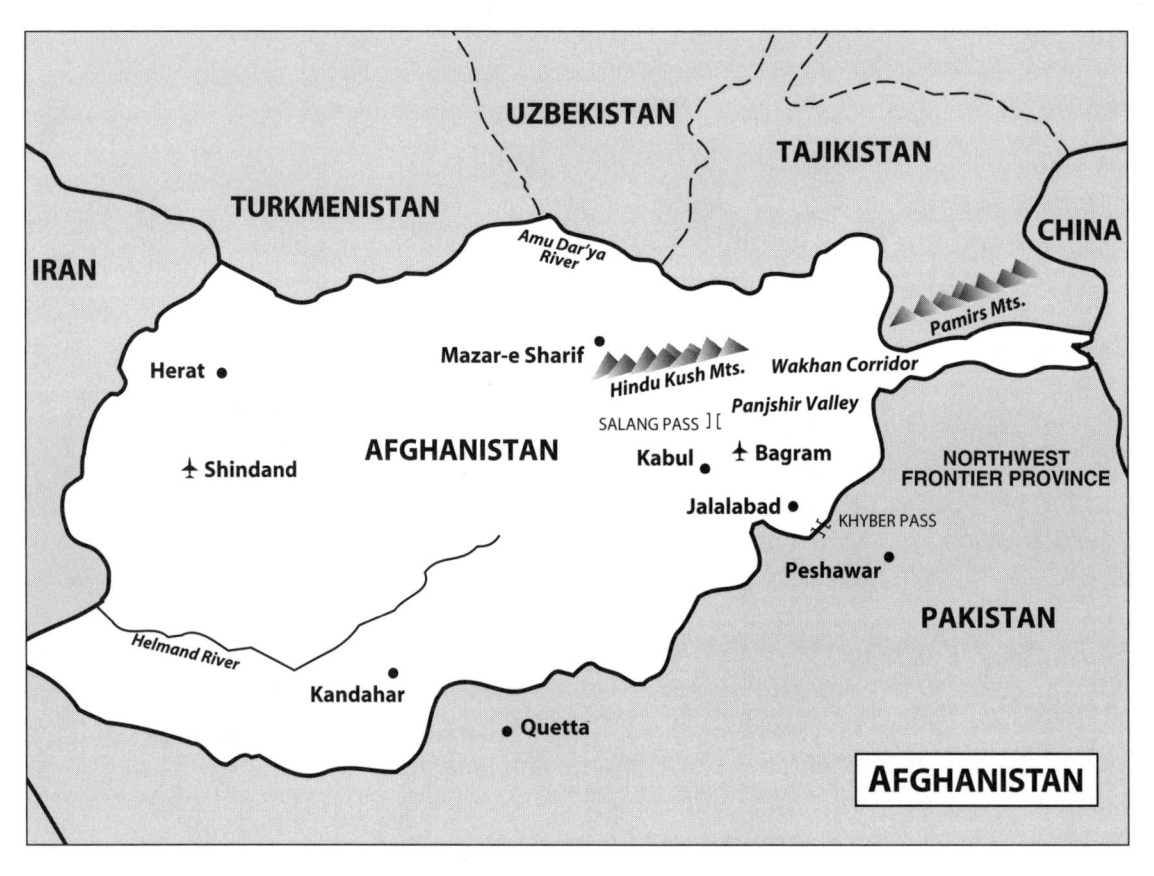

The Taliban rulers declared themselves the legitimate government. Citing Islamic law, they banned televisions, radios, and movies. Paintings, sculpture, and photography were outlawed. Women and girls were forbidden to attend school and were ordered to wear a one-piece garment called a burka, which covers the body from head to toe and has a piece of mesh built into the headdress so the wearer can see and breathe. Men were required to grow beards below the chin. Those who disobeyed these rules were publicly beaten; for more serious infractions, limbs were amputated or the offender was put to death.

When the Taliban refused to produce bin Laden after the September 11 attacks, Bush asked Congress to approve strikes against both Taliban strongholds and al-Qaeda, which is bin Laden's terrorist organization. With a Congress and nation both fearful and angry, Bush was swiftly given congressional approval.

The attacks on Afghanistan in late 2001 drove Taliban and al-Qaeda forces from major urban areas into the countryside. In November, several thousand U.S. troops entered Afghanistan to search for bin Laden as well as Taliban leader Mullah Muhammad Omar.

As 2002 began, the forces of both the Taliban and bin Laden seemed to have been defeated in Afghanistan, and Bush promised that the United States would track down the terrorist leader and also stabilize the country. It would be a difficult task at best. Right after the war, most of the cities were without water or sanitation facilities. The United Nations estimated that as many as 10 million land mines were buried throughout the countryside.

Throughout the year, sporadic fighting continued and the search for bin Laden and Omar proved fruitless. Occasionally, videotapes turned up in which the terrorist vowed to continue the fight against the United States. Each time, U.S. officials declared the tapes to be authentic.

The former king of Afghanistan, Muhammad Zahir Khan, returned to the country in mid-2002, but Afghanistan has largely reverted to control of the warlords who were in power before the Taliban took over. As of early 2004, American troops remained on duty in the country.

THE BUSH PHILOSOPHY AT WORK

Although much of the administration's time was devoted to the war against terrorism in 2002, Bush also continued to promote his philosophy of compassionate conservatism, particularly as it relates to domestic concerns. In a speech in California in 2002, Bush spoke about welfare and poverty. He said:

> Compassionate conservatism offers a new vision for fighting poverty in America. For decades America has devoted enormous resources to helping the poor, with some great successes to show for it such as medical care for those in need, a better life for elderly Americans. However, for millions of young Americans, welfare became a static and destructive way of life.[42]

He declared that time limits on welfare, job training, and work requirements can cut welfare rolls in half. He stressed that marriages and families must be strengthened through the help of charitable and religious organizations. Then he

POLICY AT HOME AND ABROAD ■ 77

spoke of a compassionate government, whether increasing international aid, helping low-income Americans to get health insurance, or reforming the Social Security laws.

Even as he spoke of a compassionate government, Bush did not abandon the conservative side of his philosophy. One area that reflected his conservatism was his policies on the environment during his first years in office. Critics charged that, from the beginning, Bush's emphasis on limited government interference in business matters has had harmful effects on the environment. They say that Bush's environmental policies have encouraged increased use of polluting, nonrenewable fossil fuels and potentially dangerous nuclear power, and that many provisions that were put in place to protect land, air, and water resources have been rolled back to accommodate big business interests. Environmentalists complained that Bush moved to stop any new legislation on environmental reforms, withdrew the United States from international environmental treaties, and underfunded the Environmental Protection Agency.

One example of Bush's environmental policy concerns oil drilling in Alaska. In the wake of the September 11 attacks, the war on terrorism, and increased instability in the Middle East, Bush repeatedly called for oil drilling in the Arctic National Wildlife Refuge. He claimed that if the oil flow from the Middle East was disrupted, the millions of barrels buried beneath the one-hundred-mile Alaskan coastal plain would compensate for the loss.

THE "NO CHILD" LAW

In January 2002, the Elementary and Secondary Education Act was passed, given the friendly name of "No Child Left Behind" (NCLB) Act by the Bush administration. Even the Democrats supported it; there is little incentive to argue with a law that seeks to raise the academic achievements of all students in the United States. The law allows states to set their own standards for Adequate Yearly Progress (AYP), which Bush claimed will keep an eye on poor schools and poor performance and be able to correct the deficiencies before children fall too far behind.

Less than two years later, critics pointed to two major faults in the law. For one thing, it was already underfunded by $8 million, with the Bush administration proposing to cut funding still further in 2004. For another, critics charged that the very fact that states can set their own standards makes it an ineffective law. They point to the state of Michigan, which lowered its passing grade in English and therefore was able to remove some thirteen hundred schools from the failing list without actually raising the academic performance of the students.

Gas prices soared in the spring of 2001. Bush advocated oil drilling in the Arctic National Wildlife Refuge as a viable solution to rising gas prices.

Congress turned down the president, in large part because environmentalists were vehemently opposed to a plan that they said would not only disturb polar-bear dens and caribou feeding grounds, but would destroy one of the most pristine and valuable wildlife lands on Earth. There was also criticism that Bush's request to drill for oil in the refuge was an attempt to help his old friends in the oil business, and that a better environmental policy would be to seek renewable sources of energy that would lessen America's dependence on foreign oil. Bush himself, however, denied the claims of cronyism and said that his policies were necessary for economic growth and for the security of the United States.

Chapter 7
Justifying War

By the beginning of his second year in office, George W. Bush had found his cause as president of the United States: removing the threat of world terrorism. On January 30, 2002, in his State of the Union address, he turned to a new front and a new war.

In a speech that startled many, especially the governments of foreign nations, he grouped the countries of Iran, Iraq, and North Korea under the heading of an "axis of evil, arming to threaten the peace of the world."[43] He warned that the war on terror was only just beginning. Russian prime minister Mikhail Kasyanov questioned what evidence Bush had for such a charge. NATO (North Atlantic Treaty Organization) warned that there would have to be solid evidence to justify any action against those nations. Other allies gave angry responses, and some voiced fears that Bush's words signaled the beginning of a new U.S. front on the war against terrorism.

But a more defiant voice was emerging from the president of the United States. Far from offering a tone of cooperation and collaboration with America's allies, Bush simply maintained his tough stance and said that "all the three countries I mentioned are now on notice that we intend to take their development of weapons of mass destruction very seriously."[44] In a departure from previous government leadership, it looked as though the Bush administration had decided to follow a path to war regardless of the concerns and/or objections of its allies.

Even with bin Laden still at large and the problems of Afghanistan unsolved, Bush soon sought to convince a majority of the American people to go to war against the nation of Iraq and tried to justify his actions to other world powers. This shift in direction drew attention away from Afghanistan and caused his critics to wonder where the initiative for stabilizing that country and removing the threat of terror had gone. It also greatly increased America's financial commitment to war. Reportedly, the national surplus left after the Clinton administration had already disappeared, and for the first time, the president's high approval rating started a small downward turn. But Bush was determined to continue in what he regarded as a justifiable crusade to rid the world of terrorism.

A History of Trouble

One of Bush's key points for justifying war against the Islamic country of Iraq was its reported possession of weapons of mass destruction. Iraq had been having disputes with the United Nations about that issue for some time. Located at the northwestern end of the Persian Gulf, Iraq has a history that reaches back as early as 3500 B.C. Once known as Mesopotamia, it was a battleground for centuries and was occupied by the British during World War I. A monarchy was established in 1921 and full independence achieved in 1932. Military coups followed one after the other until the socialist Baath Party took over in 1968. One of that party's leaders was Saddam Hussein. He held power in the country with President Ahmad Hassan al-Bakr and directed the nationalization of Iraq's oil industry in 1972. When Bakr resigned in 1979, Hussein assumed full power. He was able to industrialize the country and improve social services while keeping tight and brutal autocratic control. Iraq invaded neighboring Iran in 1980, starting a war that was ended by a cease-fire in 1988. When Hussein invaded neighboring Kuwait in 1990, a coalition led by the United States during the administration of the elder Bush was victorious in stopping the invasion, but it did not remove the dictator from office.

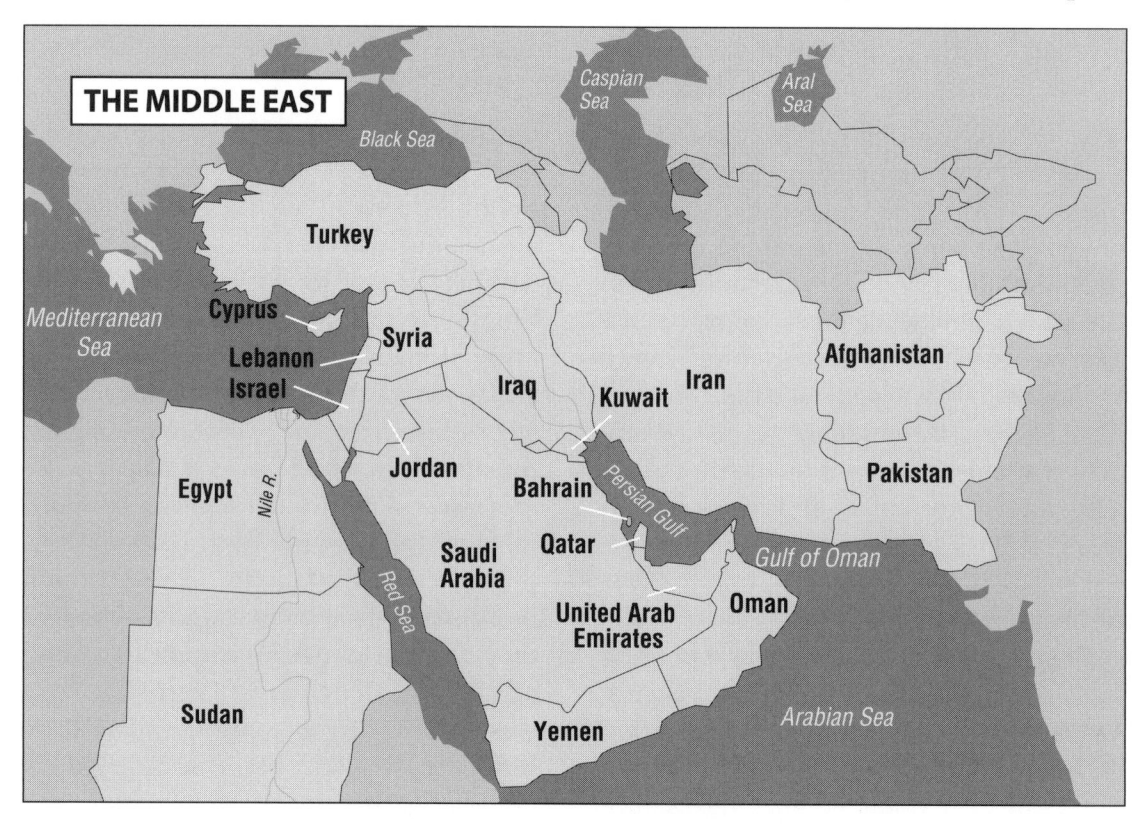

In 1991, the United Nations ordered Hussein to stop the production of weapons of mass destruction and to allow a UN special commission to conduct inspections to see that its order was carried out. Over the next several years, friction developed between Hussein's government and UN inspectors. Iraq demanded that the inspectors leave, and they were denied access to military sites.

THE TICKING WAR BOMB

Bush started the war bomb ticking over Iraq when he addressed the United Nations on September 12, 2002, presenting a case against Hussein's continued opposition to UN inspectors. Shortly afterward, the Iraqi government allowed the inspectors back in. A few days later, British prime minister Tony Blair stated that Iraq had the capacity to produce a nuclear weapon in about two years if it got the material and other components from abroad.

Bush began to be more and more visible during this period, and with every opportunity, he talked of a possible confrontation with Hussein. Citing reports of the Iraqi government's atrocities on its people, Bush called Hussein an evil and brutal dictator. With each speech or each report of Iraq's continued resistance to UN inspectors, Bush seemed to grow more and more confident and determined in his newfound direction. On October 10, Bush asked for and received from the U.S. Congress a resolution to use armed force against the Republic of Iraq. He signed the resolution on October 16.

When Iraq published a report later in 2002 saying it had long ago abandoned a program to produce a nuclear weapon, the White House, through Secretary of State Colin Powell, hinted that it would reject such an assertion. However, by the end of the year, the UN inspection teams had found no weapons of mass destruction.

Early in 2003 it was growing increasingly clear that the president of the United States was determined to wage war, with or without the aid or even the sanction of other nations. He was furious when France and Germany suggested tripling the number of inspectors and even backing them up with surveillance flights. Bush now believed that the only way to rid the world of what he regarded as an imminent threat to world peace was his way—invading Iraq and forcing Hussein from power.

Bush's cause was not helped in February when Hans Blix, head of the UN inspection operation, said that Iraq was cooperating to some extent with the inspections and that there was no clear cause for war at that time. As antiwar protestors gathered in cities around the world, the U.S. government struck a deal that would allow its troops to be deployed in Turkey in the event of war. But the Bush administration was given a setback when the Turkish parliament rejected the plan.

On March 6, 2003, Bush addressed the American people and said that war was very close. Two weeks later, he met with Blair to give the United Nations twenty-four hours to enforce a disarmament of Iraq, or forces consisting primarily of American and British troops would invade the country. (In fact, Great Britain became the only

Iraqi schoolgirls walk past U.S. soldiers preparing to storm the home of a Saddam Hussein loyalist in 2003. American troops in Iraq encountered fierce resistance.

major ally of the United States.) Russia, France, Germany, and China announced their refusal to join such a military action despite Powell's requests for their help.

WAR IN IRAQ

Bush's administration grew more and more focused on ousting Hussein. It was a sentiment in some ways left over from his father's administration and the Gulf War. Vice President Cheney had served under the elder Bush, and like many others in that administration felt that the war had not been entirely successful because Hussein had not been removed from power. In fact, after Cheney became vice president, he told an aide concerning Iraq, "We have swept the problem under the rug for too long. We have a festering problem there."[45]

Bush gave Hussein an ultimatum on March 18: leave Iraq within forty-eight hours or face invasion. Bush was convinced of the necessity of his action for three main reasons: One, he believed that Iraq was hiding weapons of mass destruction. Two, after the attacks on September 11, conservatives in the government presented the thought that if members of bin Laden's al-Qaeda group acquired any Iraqi weapons of mass destruction, the entire free world would suffer. (However, there was no evidence linking al-Qaeda to Hussein.) Third, an invasion would rid the country of a brutal dictator.

The war against the nation of Iraq began on March 20, 2003. Soon after the deadline passed without response from Iraq, U.S. planes began to bomb Baghdad, the capital city. A succession of massive air strikes was planned, according to the U.S. military, to "shock and awe"[46] Iraq's military into giving up. China, France, and Russia immediately denounced the action.

While antiwar protests continued around the world, the war in Iraq went on, but by late April, it was evident that U.S. military might would prevail, even though fighting proved more difficult than had been anticipated. The administration had been confident that the

THE CRUELEST DICTATOR

Before America's war on Iraq in 2003, Saddam Hussein had spent two decades as president of that Islamic nation during which time he became one of the most hated Arab leaders in the world and feared by his own people. He was born outside of Tikrit, Iraq, in April 1937, and joined the Baath Party when he went to college in Baghdad. The monarchy in Iraq was overthrown in 1958, and when Hussein's conspiracy to kill the prime minister was discovered, he was expelled from the country. By 1963, the Baath Party was in control, so Hussein returned home. However, the party was out again within months, and Hussein was in jail until the party returned to power in 1968. With his position on the ruling Revolutionary Command Council, Hussein was the power behind the ailing president, Ahmed Hassam Bakr. By 1979, Hussein himself was head of state. He immediately had all his rivals put to death.

Throughout his years in power until ousted by the Iraq war in 2003, Hussein used chemical weapons, terror, and brutality against any enemies and even his own people. When questioned by reporters about his tactics through the years, the dictator has calmly replied that he had no other choice in order to hold together such a vast and diverse country. And, despite his reprehensible tactics, some still regard him as a hero, an Arab who dared to stand up to the nations of the West.

oppressed Iraqis would eagerly embrace the American troops, but such was not always the case, and fighting was especially fierce in the south. In early April, U.S. marines entered Baghdad, but Hussein was nowhere to be found.

Bush urged the United Nations to lift economic sanctions against Iraq that had been imposed on the country thirteen years earlier. He declared Iraq to be liberated, although fighting continued in some areas, and looting and lawlessness were rampant. On May 1, he told the American public that major combat operations in Iraq had ended. The statement proved to be premature, for continuing through the year came almost daily reports of American deaths either from sniper attacks, bombs, or rocket-propelled grenades. The U.S. death toll after May 1 climbed past the figure of American fatalities during the short declared war. American dead and wounded from the beginning of the war until late in the year totaled about twenty-five hundred. On October 29, 2003, it was reported that more Americans had been killed in Iraq after May 1 than during the official war.

Near the end of 2003, the chaos in Baghdad continued. One of the most horrific acts occurred on October 27 when powerful suicide car bombs exploded outside the local headquarters of the International Committee of the Red Cross, killing at least thirty-four people, including one U.S. soldier, and wounding 224. This was the worst such attack since Hussein's government was toppled but well into the year 2004, the attacks continue.

THE USA PATRIOT ACT

In addition to facing questions about the continued unrest in Iraq, the Bush administration also faced questions about civil rights at home. When Bush spoke of a war against terror by the United States in 2002, he already had some new legal authority behind him. Congress had responded to the country's grief and anger over the attacks on the World Trade Center and the Pentagon on September 11, 2001, by hastily passing the USA PATRIOT Act less than two months later, on October 24. Its purpose was "to deter and punish terrorist acts in the United States and around the world, to enhance law enforcement investigatory tools, and for other purposes."[47]

The act gave sweeping new changes to the government in the areas of surveillance procedures such as intercepting wire and electronic communications and access to personal records. The president was given the authority to authorize taking property and possessions from those whom the government judges as engaging in hostile acts against the U.S. government.

Although the Patriot Act was passed in a fervor of antiterrorist emotions, by 2003, people in and out of the government were taking a closer look at the authority given to the government and the possible infringement on civil rights. Early in the year, it was rumored that the so-called USA PATRIOT Act Part II was being considered by Attorney General John Ashcroft and his staff. At year's end, this bill, now called the Benjamin Franklin Patriots Act, was on the House calendar. Civil rights groups, such as the American Civil Liberties Union (ACLU), promised a fight to keep it from becoming law. They charged that the new act strikes a deeper blow at civil rights. It would remove existing protections of privacy now guaranteed under the Freedom of Information Act and make it easier for the government to hide people it wishes to detain. Critics charge that the most troubling section would take away U.S. citizenship from any person who

President Bush appeals to the United Nations to sanction his war on terrorism. Many have criticized Bush for waging war on Iraq without UN support.

JUSTIFYING WAR ■ 87

Demonstrators protest the USA PATRIOT Act passed after the September 11, 2001, terrorist attacks. Critics believe that the act violates civil rights protections.

gives "material support" to any group designated by the attorney general as a terrorist organization.

While Bush has long claimed that such laws as the Patriot Act are needed in a time of rampant terrorism, critics say he is heading an administration that has become drunk on power and supports secrecy at all costs.

The Warlike Aftermath

In the halls of Congress, in the continued fighting and death in Iraq, and in other regions of the world that have suffered violence, the war on terror remains a major problem to Bush and his administration. Many Democrats and Republicans alike who early on supported his efforts to rid the world of Hussein began to find fault with an administration that they claim had no policy for dealing with the occupation of Iraq after the official war ended. That, coupled with the prospect of a long U.S. occupation costing many billions of dollars, plus no evidence of weapons of mass destruction and no sight of the Iraqi dictator, had by late fall—and for the first time since he took office—dropped approval ratings to below 50 percent.

But Bush refused to budge in the face of grumblings from Congress, discontent among the American people, and outright hostility from foreign powers. He declared that his policy in Iraq will restructure the nation into a peaceful democracy. His requests for aid from other countries in settling the peace have, however, for the most part fallen on deaf ears. He spoke before the United Nations in October 2003 urging other nations to join the United States in its efforts to restore peace to Iraq. But UN members, still angry over Bush's arrogant "go-it-alone" policy, say they will help to rebuild Iraq only if leadership is shared. Bush has so far refused to relinquish American power in Iraq.

In late October 2003, Bush asked the U.S. Congress for $87 billion to spend on restoring peace to Iraq. Members of Congress at first said they would refuse the request unless it was made in the form of a loan, which Bush rejected, but the request was passed in November.

The Economy After All

While Bush was busy directing the war in Iraq, changes were occurring in the American economy that could seriously impact his chances for reelection. And the circumstances were strangely like his father's first and only term. When the elder Bush had campaigned for the presidency in 1989, his famous pledge was "Read my lips, no new taxes." During his term, however, the economy stalled and unemployment rose. Through a lingering recession—a downward trend in the business cycle characterized by a decline in production and employment—more businesses failed than at any time in the United States since the Great Depression of the 1930s. The budget deficit soared to $350 billion, and the elder Bush was forced to agree to tax hikes despite his campaign pledge. In 1990, he ordered Allied troops into Iraq in response to Iraq's invasion of Kuwait. That increased his approval rating to 89 percent, but as the economy floundered, his ratings dropped and dropped. With his ratings down, Bush was defeated by Bill Clinton and went home after one term in the White House.

Bush is in a situation much like his father's. In his first term, the elder Bush also sent American troops to Iraq, for which he received a very high approval rating. But the economy began to suffer, and his ratings began to drop. By early 2004, political experts believed that the administration's success or failure in Iraq would be overshadowed in the voting polls by a rise or fall in the economy, which shows only limited recovery. Bush got a boost in December 2003, when U.S. forces captured Saddam Hussein.

The midwestern state of Illinois is a good example of how Bush's reelection hangs on the outcome of these two events: In the 2000 election, Illinois went Democratic by a wide margin. But after the attacks of September 11 and after Bush began to show an assertive side in his handling of the crisis and reassurances to the nation, Illinois voters began to warm up to him, Democrats and Republicans alike. His approval rating soon hit 57 percent, which is very high for a largely Democratic state. However, by the end of 2003, that rating had dropped to 46 percent, and 44 percent of Illinois voters disapproved of the way he was handling the job.

Bush's answer to the troubled economy has always been a tax cut. Many experts agree with him, but many do not. According to his economic theory, a tax cut is intended to put money into the private sector, taking it away from the federal government and thereby stimulating the economy. The Republican Party in general believes that too much of the nation's wealth is concentrated in the federal government. They believe that if people have more money in their pockets, they will spend it, not put it away. Spending money makes businesses grow and creates jobs. But the tax cuts ordered by the Bush administration have not had that desired effect, some say because the amount for each person is so small that it stimulates nothing.

The most troubling part of the sluggish economy to Illinois was the unemployment rate in late 2003. It stood at 7.1 percent, the highest of all the states. Nationwide, the unemployment rate was 6.1 percent, the highest since 1988. Bush is certain to keep his eyes on the unemployment rate and the economy in general as he seeks reelection in september.

FAMILY IN AND OUT OF THE WHITE HOUSE

Faced with trouble abroad and a wobbly economy, the president of the United States finds little time to keep in touch with his family members. But they still sustain him in a crisis: he talks frequently with his mother and father, less so with his four brothers and his sister.

Even so, George W. and Laura Bush try to maintain a close family life in the unrelenting glare of the presidential spotlight. It was never easy for any president to do so before the terrorist attacks,

President Bush greets Secret Service agents. Constantly accompanied by agents, Bush sometimes finds it challenging to maintain a normal family life.

but it is even more difficult now with always-tight security even tighter around the chief executive and family. Months after the attack on September 11, Bush was able to recall events that evening with a certain amount of humor. He said that after a small argument with the Secret Service about going to sleep in their own residential quarters in the White House (the Secret Service wanted a safer site), Bush recalled that the Secret Service came to get them about 11:30 P.M., saying that an unidentified aircraft was heading toward the White House: "So we get out of bed. I'm actually in my running shorts with a t-shirt, old shoes. Grab Barney, grab Spot (the family dogs). Laura has no contacts, so she's holding on to my arm. We get to the elevator and straight down. . . . Then an enlisted fellow walks into the briefing room and goes, 'Mr. President, good news! It's one of our own!'"[48]

Except for such unusual happenings, the president and first lady maintain a low-key, informal-as-possible lifestyle in the White House. Bush's 250 baseballs have a niche of their own, the twins have rooms when they come in from the University of Texas and Yale, and the small second-floor kitchen for the family is stocked with Bush favorites of egg salad, peanut butter, and jelly. Most of their entertaining is informal, given to barbecuing, except for formal state dinners. When not entertaining dignitaries, the Bushes keep to their normal routine; he gets up at 6 A.M. and feeds the pets. In the evening they watch television—lots of sports and action films. They usually retire by 10 P.M. Wrote *Washington Post* society reporter Roxanne Roberts, "They're . . . just like your next-door neighbor."[49]

Epilogue

The Next Journey

The next political journey of George W. Bush—his reelection campaign—will either send him back to the White House or home to Texas in 2004. As he headed into the year, he was faced with an unsolved problem in Afghanistan, escalating unrest in Iraq and the Middle East, and a national economy problem that would not go away. However, political experts say all it would take for an easy Bush reelection would be for the fighting to stop in Iraq and the economy to stop drifting.

Bush is a far more confident man today than when he first stepped into the Oval Office. Out of the shadow of his father, he asserts himself and his policies with an attitude that has changed from youthfully cocky to near-studied defiance. If he is unsure of himself, it no longer shows. This new confidence, however, has polarized the public for and against him. The somewhat unsure leader who spoke to the citizens the evening of September 11, 2001, and who seemed to gain stature as the days wore on was easy for most people to rally around. With his newfound confidence, he registered reassurance to a nation that was deeply stunned by the unthinkable atrocity of having its homeland violated.

However, as time has pushed the terrorist attacks more and more into the background and voters are faced with uncertainty about war and unrest overseas and a failing economy, Bush is being viewed in a more discerning light. In order to avoid his father's fate as a one-time president, he must bring the peace to Iraq that he insists will come because he has removed from power an evil dictator and he must stabilize an economy that stubbornly refuses to follow his will. How he fares on these two issues will more than likely decide whether he spends four more years in the White House or goes back to his Texas ranch.

Yet, even if he spends only four years as the chief executive, George W. Bush has made an impact on the role of the U.S. presidency. Not in recent history has an American leader been so willing to go it alone in world affairs. He has adopted a policy of "America leads and the world follows," and he either cannot or will not retreat from it. He is also convinced that his policy of compassionate conservatism is the only path for America to follow. This new outlook extends to the president's relationship with Congress as well. The opposition has commented on a spirit of combativeness rather than conciliation between the two parties that dominate the Washington political scene.

So far, America's allies, with the exception of the British government, have remained entrenched in their determination not to walk in lockstep with the policies of the Bush administration. Unless there is give on one side or both, Bush and the American people could find themselves shouldering an intolerable psychological and financial burden to bring peace to Iraq and the Middle East.

An example of European resentment against the Bush policies occurred in November 2003 when the president visited Great Britain, his only major partner in the Iraqi war. When the proposed trip was first announced, there were plans by the British government for a full-scale celebration of the president's arrival, including a ceremonial ride with Queen Elizabeth in her royal carriage. Shortly before Bush and the first lady flew to London, however, much of the highly visible celebrating was cancelled

Bush is confident that his achievements during his first term in office together with his vision for the future will win him a second presidential term.

to avoid the embarrassment of thousands of antiwar protestors rallying against the president and his policies in Iraq. Acknowledging the opposition in European countries, Bush took the opportunity to speak to the British people and, in effect, to the people of Europe as well. He encouraged the governments of Europe to rally behind his long-term campaign to defeat terrorism. He was defiant against the criticism leveled at him by opponents and not only tried to justify his decision to go to war with Iraq but sought to prepare the rest of the world for the possibility that the United States might go into combat again if faced with what the government considered an obvious evil.

Time will show whether Bush's philosophy of compassionate conservatism works for America and whether this change in the role of the U.S. president is a permanent one. With his newfound sense of authority and security in himself, his family, and his religion, George W. Bush is certain he has four more years to prove himself correct.

Notes

Introduction: Terror Hits Home

1. Quoted in CNN.com, "September 11: Chronology of Terror," September 12, 2001. www.cnn.com.
2. Quoted in David Frum, *The Right Man: The Surprise Presidency of George W. Bush*. New York: Random House, 2003.

Chapter 1: A Strong Family Bond

3. Quoted in Bill Minutaglio, *First Son: George W. Bush and the Bush Family Dynasty*. New York: Random House, 1999, p. 25.
4. Quoted in Minutaglio, *First Son*, p. 27.
5. Quoted in Amy Cunningham, "Good-Bye to Robin," *Texas Monthly*, February 1988, pp. 80–82.
6. Quoted in Minutaglio, *First Son*, p. 47.
7. Quoted in *Time*, "The Quiet Dynasty," August 7, 2000, p. 40.
8. Quoted in Minutaglio, *First Son*, p. 48.
9. Quoted in Minutaglio, *First Son*, p. 58.
10. Quoted in Helen Thorpe, "Go East, Young Man," *Texas Monthly*, June 1999, p. 107
11. Quoted in Thorpe, "Go East, Young Man," p. 107.

Chapter 2: Later School Years

12. Quoted in "The Quiet Dynasty," p. 40.
13. Quoted in Thorpe, "Go East, Young Man," p. 107.
14. Quoted in Thorpe, "Go East, Young Man," p. 107.
15. Quoted in Elizabeth Mitchell, *W: Revenge of the Bush Dynasty*. New York: Hyperion, 2000, p. 109.
16. Quoted in Minutaglio, *First Son*, p. 117.
17. Quoted in Minutaglio, *First Son*, p. 141.

Chapter 3: The Businessman from Texas

18. George W. Bush, *A Charge to Keep*. New York: Morrow, 1999, p. 130.
19. Quoted in Mitchell, *W*, p. 164.
20. Bush, *A Charge to Keep*, p. 136.
21. Quoted in Mitchell, *W*, p. 203.
22. Quoted in Minutaglio, *First Son*, p. 210.
23. Quoted in Evan Smith, "George, Washington," *Texas Monthly*, June 1999, p. 111.
24. Quoted in Mitchell, *W*, p. 252.
25. Quoted in Joe Nick, "Team Player," "*Texas Monthly*, June 1999, p. 113.

Chapter 4: In the Governor's Seat

26. Quoted in Mitchell, *W*, p. 294.
27. Quoted in Howard Fineman, "Lone Star Rising," *Newsweek*, April 21, 1997, p. 30.

Chapter 5: The Disputed Election

28. Quoted in Fineman, "Lone Star Rising," p. 30.
29. Quoted in Ian Christopher McCaleb and Mike Ferullo, "Bush Calls for Renewal of Civility, Implementation of 'Compassionate Conservatism,'" CNN.com. www.cnn.com.
30. Quoted in McCaleb and Ferullo, "Bush Calls for Renewal,"
31. Quoted in *Newsweek*, "What a Long, Strange Trip," November 20, 2000, p. 30.
32. Quoted in "What a Long, Strange Trip," p. 30.
33. Quoted in *Newsmakers*, "Jeb Bush," September 9, 2003. http://galenet.galegroup.com.

34. Quoted in "Jeb Bush."

Chapter 6: Policy at Home and Abroad

35. Quoted in Howard Fineman, "A President Faces the Test of a Lifetime," *Newsweek*, September 13, 2001, p. 32.
36. Quoted in Fineman, "A President Faces the Test of a Lifetime," p. 32.
37. *Time*, "Bush in the Crucible," September 24, 2001, p. 48.
38. Quoted in "Bush in the Crucible," p. 48.
39. Quoted in Michael C. Dorf, "Why Congressional Powers to Declare War Do Not Provide an Effective Check on the President," March 6, 2002. http://writ.news.findlaw.com.
40. Quoted in the White House. www.whitehouse.gov.
41. Quoted in U.S. Department of State "The White House." http://usinfo.state.gov.
42. Quoted in The White House, "President Promotes Compassionate Conservatism," April 2002. www.whitehouse.gov.

Chapter 7: Justifying War

43. Quoted in Michael Elliott and James Carney, "First Stop, Iraq," *Time*, March 31, 2003, p. 172.
44. Quoted in BBC NEWS. http://news.bbc.co.uk.
45. Quoted in Elliott and Carney, "First Stop, Iraq," p. 172.
46. Quoted in Elliott and Carney, "First Stop, Iraq, p. 172.
47. Quoted in Electronic Privacy Information Center. www.epic.org.
48. Quoted in *PR Newswire*, "Newsweek Exclusive Interview: President George W. and Laura Bush," November 25, 2001, p. 216.
49. Quoted in *People Weekly*, "The First Lady Next Door," January 29, 2001, p. 50.

For Further Reading

Books

Jann Armbuster, *United Nations*. New York: Watts, 1997. Describes the function and daily operation of this peacekeeping organization.

Gloria Blake, *Condoleezza Rice*. New York: Chelsea House, 2004. A close-up portrait of the president's national security adviser.

Rose Blue and Corinne J. Naden, *People of Peace*. Brookfield, CT: Millbrook, 1994. Profiles of people who have devoted their lives to bringing about peace in the world.

Daniel Cohen, *George W. Bush: The Family Business*. Brookfield, CT: Millbrook, 2000. The family business is politics; the story of the Bush dynasty.

Deanne Durrett, *George W. Bush*. San Diego: KidHaven, 2003. From a childhood in Texas to a home in the White House; the political history of George W. Bush.

Beatrice Gormley, *Laura Bush—America's First Lady*. New York: Aladdin, 2003. Describes the personality of the quiet, confident woman who prefers to be out of the spotlight.

Vida Boyd Jones, *George W. Bush*. New York: Chelsea House, 2003. A straightforward biography of the forty-third president.

Works Consulted

Books

Frank Bruni, *Ambling into History: The Unlikely Odyssey of George W. Bush.* New York: Harper, 2002. A behind-the-scenes look at Bush's often-chronicled weaknesses and sometimes overlooked strengths.

George W. Bush, *A Charge to Keep.* New York: Morrow, 1999. The personal and political experiences that led Bush to make a decision to run for the presidency.

David Frum, *The Right Man: The Surprise Presidency of George W. Bush.* New York: Random House, 2003. An inside account of a historic year in the Bush White House.

Molly Ivins and Lou DuBose, *Shrub: The Short but Happy Political Life of George W. Bush.* New York: Random House, 2003. A perceptive and entertaining analysis that gets to the heart of Bush's policies and motivations.

David Kaplan, *The Accidental President.* New York: Morrow, 2001. Details of the bizarre 2000 election that got Bush into the White House.

Bill Minutaglio, *First Son: George W. Bush and the Bush Family Dynasty.* New York: Random House, 1999. The story of the power and politics of the Bush dynasty.

Elizabeth Mitchell, *W: Revenge of the Bush Dynasty.* New York: Hyperion, 2000. What Bush learned from his father on his way to becoming president.

Periodicals

Phillips Andrew, "The Bush League," *MacClean's*, November 16, 1998.

Stephen Andrew, "The Day That Nobody Would Take Charge," *New Statesman*, September 17, 2001.

Jeffrey H. Birnbaum, "The Man Who Could Be President," *Fortune*, March 29, 1999.

Rich Blake, "Make Room for Marvin," *Institutional Investor*, May 2000.

Martha Brant, "Comforter in Chief," *Newsweek*, December 3, 2001.

Paul Burka, "George W. Bush and the New Political Landscape," *Texas Monthly*, December 1994.

Amy Cunningham, "Good-Bye to Robin," *Texas Monthly*, February 1988.

Economist, "The Accidental President," December 16, 2000.

Michael Elliott and James Carney, "First Stop, Iraq," *Time*, March 31, 2003.

Howard Fineman, "Bush and God," *Newsweek*, March 10, 2003.

———, "Harkening Back to Texas," *Newsweek*, June 22, 2002.

———, "Lone Star Rising," *Newsweek*, April 21, 1997.

———, "A President Faces the Test of a Lifetime," *Newsweek*, September 13, 2001.

Fred I. Greenstein "The Contemporary Presidency," *Presidential Studies Quarterly*, June 2002.

Stephen J. Hedges, "The Color of Money," *U.S. News & World Report*, March 16, 1992.

Skip Hollandsworth, "Born to Run: What's in a Name," *Texas Monthly*, May 1994.

———, "The Many Faces of George W. Bush," *Texas Monthly*, February 1995.

Mark Hosenball, "The Brothers Bush: Would You Buy a Used Car from These Guys?" *New Republic*, April 3, 1989.

Richard Jerome, "Here Comes the Son," *People Weekly*, August 7, 2000.

Newsweek, "A Son's Restless Journey," August 7, 2000.

———, "What a Long, Strange Trip," November 20, 2000.

———, "Where There's Smoke," March 26, 2001.

New York Times Upfront, "The Final Moves," December 11, 2000.

Joe Nick, "Team Player," *Texas Monthly*, June 1999.

People Weekly, "The First Lady Next Door," January 29, 2001.

PR Newswire, "Friends Say President's Daughter Barbara Likes to Party Like Her Twin," June 3, 2001.

———, "Newsweek Exclusive Interview: President George W. Bush and Laura Bush," November 25, 2001.

Michael Scherer, "That Other Bush Boy," *Mother Jones*, May/June 2001.

Hugh Side, "I Made a Mistake, I Went Too Far," *Time*, August 14, 2000.

Roger Simon et al., "Eyes on the Prize," *U.S. News & World Report*, November 27, 2000.

Evan Smith, "George, Washington," *Texas Monthly*, June 1999.

Jill Smolowe et al., "Double Trouble," *People Weekly*, June 18, 2001.

———, "What $6 Million Can Buy," *Time*, January 28, 2002.

Helen Thorpe, "Go East, Young Man," *Texas Monthly*, June 1999.

Time, "Bush in the Crucible," September 24, 2001.

———, "The Quiet Dynasty," August 7, 2002.

Kenneth T. Walsh, "The Man from Midland," *U.S. News & World Report*, June 7, 1999.

Internet Sources

CNN.com "September 11: Chronology of Terror," September 12, 2001. www.cnn.com.

Michael C. Dorf, "Why Congressional Powers to Declare War Do Not Provide an Effective Check on the President," March 6, 2002. http://writ.news.findlaw.com.

Electronic Privacy Information Center. www.epic.org.

The Handbook of Texas Online, "Kinkaid School." www.tsha.utexas.edu.

———, "Texas Rangers." www.tsha.utexas.edu.

Ian Christopher McCaleb and Mike Ferullo,

"Bush Calls for Renewal of Civility, Implementation of 'Compassionate Conservatism,'" CNN.com. www.cnn.com.

Phillips Academy Andover, "About Andover." www.andover.edu.

Texas State Library and Archives Commission, "Ann W. Richards, Portraits of Texas Governors." www.tsl.state.tx.us.

U.S. Department of State, "The White House." http://usinfo.state.gov.

The White House, "President Promotes Compassionate Conservatism," April 2002. www.whitehouse.gov.

Index

Afghanistan, 75–77, 81
Air Force One (aircraft), 70, 71–73
Allbaugh, Joseph, 57
Andover (academy), 22–23, 24, 32
Arbusto, 37–38, 39
  see also oil business
Arctic National Wildlife Refuge, 78, 80
Ashcroft, John, 86
Atwater, Lee, 43
"axis of evil," 81

Benjamin Franklin Patriots Act, 86–87
Betts, Roland, 47
bin Laden, Osama, 74, 75
Blair, Tony, 83
Buchanan, Pat, 66
Bush, Barbara Pierce (daughter), 39, 49, 56, 66
Bush, Barbara Pierce (mother)
  background of, 13
  on grieving death of daughter, 16
  relationship of, with George W. Bush, 16, 20, 44–45, 58
Bush, Dorothy, 19
Bush, George Herbert Walker
  background of, 13
  Central Intelligence Agency and, 33
  China and, 33
  economic problems during presidency of, 89–90
  election losses of, 24–25, 30
  election of, to Congress, 25
  presidency of, 42–43
  on raising taxes, 89
  Republican Party and, 33
  vice presidency of, 37–38
  World War II heroism of, 17
Bush, George W.
  abortion policy of, 51–52
  academic performance of, 24, 25
  acceptance speech of, 59
  alcohol and, 25, 30, 32, 37, 40
  athletic competition and, 16–17, 20
  aviation and, 29–30
  baseball and, 44–47, 49
  big business interests and, 61–62
  birth of, 13

on Bush family characteristics, 37
capital punishment and, 53
challenges facing, 93–95
childhood of, 15–19
college years of, 24–28
communication style of, 69, 73, 74
election loss of, 36–37
election of, as governor of Texas, 48–49
energy level of, 23, 49
family life of, 90, 92
family tradition and, 13
future of, 93–95
governorship of Texas and, 49–54
on his mother, 16
leadership style of, 68
marriage of, 34–35
military service of, 29–30
nomination of, for president, 56–58
patriotism and, 70
personality of, 54
political instincts of, 20, 25, 30, 36–37, 43–44, 47
prison reform and, 52
racism and, 53
on relationship with father, 29
relationship of, with mother, 16, 20, 45, 58
relationship of, with siblings, 19
religion and, 40–42
on religious conversion, 40
on security of family, 92
work experience of, 24, 37–40, 44–47
Bush, Jenna Welch, 39, 49, 56, 66
Bush, John Ellis ("Jeb"), 15, 63, 67
Bush, Laura Welch
background of, 33, 34
politics and, 35, 37
role of, 37, 68
Bush, Marvin, 17
Bush, Neil, 17
Bush, Pauline Robinson ("Robin"), 15–16
Bush, Prescott Sheldon, 13
Bush Exploration Company, 39
see also oil business

cabinet, 68
Cheney, Richard (Dick), 9, 59, 84–85
Christian conservatives, 52–53
Clinton, Bill, 59, 61
compassionate conservatism, 12, 51, 57, 77–78
conservatism, 12, 51

economic policies, 90
see also tax policies
education policies,

19–20, 22–23, 49, 51, 73, 78
election of 2000, 8, 59–67
environmental policies, 57, 78, 80

Florida, 63–67
foreign policy, 93–95
  see also
    Afghanistan; "axis of evil"; Iraq; war on terror
fundraising, 61–62

Giuliani, Rudolph, 11
Gore, Al
  Clinton association and, 61, 62–63
  election loss statistics for, 8
  election night 2000 and, 63–64
  leadership and political experience of, 61, 62–63
  postelection struggles of, 67
Graham, Billy, 40

Ground Zero. *See* September 11, 2001

Hannah, Doug, 20
Harken Energy Corporation, 39, 43
  see also oil business
Harris, Katherine, 66
Harvard Business School, 31, 32–33
Houston, Texas, 19
Hughes, Karen, 57, 73
Hussein, Saddam, 82, 83, 85

immigration policies, 53
inauguration, 67
Iran, 81
Iraq
  arguments for and against war with, 83–84, 89
  "axis of evil" and, 81
  history summary of, 82–83
  United Nations and, 82–83
  war with, 85–86
  weapons of mass destruction and, 82, 83

Johnson, Clay, 23

Kasyanov, Mikhail, 81
Khan, Muhammad Zahir, 77
Kinkaid School, 19–20
Kuwait, 82

liberalism, 51
Lieberman, Joseph, 59, 61
literacy, 35, 51

Mack, Connie, 59
Mallon, Neil, 26
McCain, John, 57–58
Middle East. *See* Afghanistan; Iraq; war on terror
Minutaglio, Bill, 30
Mitchell, Elizabeth, 37

Newsweek (magazine), 73

"No Child Left Behind" (NCLB) Act, 78
North Atlantic Treaty Organization (NATO), 81
North Korea, 81

oil business, 15, 33, 37–40, 53, 78
Omar, Mohammad, 76

Pentagon. *See* September 11, 2001
Phillips Academy, 22–23, 24, 32
philosophy, 12, 51–54, 77–78
 see also compassionate conservatism; religion
Pioneers, 61–62
Powell, Colin, 59, 68, 83
presidency, 12, 93–94
Professionals United for Leadership (PULL), 32

al-Qaeda, 77, 85
Quayle, Dan, 42–43

Rangers (baseball team), 44–47
Reagan, Ronald, 38–39
Reeves, Jim, 46
religion, 40–42
Rice, Condoleezza, 9, 68
Richards, Ann, 48–49
Roberts, Roxanne, 92
Robertson, Pat, 53
Rose, Edward, 44
Rove, Karl, 57, 70
Rumsfeld, Donald, 9, 68

September 11, 2001
 aftermath of, 70–74
 civil rights impact of, 86–88
 foreign policy and, 93–95
 summary of events of, 8–12, 70
 see also war on terror
Skull and Bones Society, 25, 26
Spectrum 7, 39
 see also oil business
Staudt, Walter B., 29

Taliban, 75–77
tax policies, 51, 53, 69, 90
Texas Rangers (baseball team), 44–47
Texas Reading Initiative, 51
Time (magazine), 73
Tucker, Karla Faye, 53

Ueberroth, Peter, 44
USA PATRIOT Act, 86–89

war on terror
 Afghanistan and, 75–77
 arguments for and against, 89
 civil rights and, 86–88
 development of,

74–75
foreign policy and, 93–95
legal impact of, 86–89
see also "axis of evil"; September 11, 2001

Washington Post (newspaper), 92
welfare reform, 49, 51, 77–78

World Trade Center. *See* September 11, 72001

Yale University, 24, 25–27

Picture Credits

Cover: © Brooks Craft/ CORBIS
© AFP/Corbis, 55, 60, 63, 72
© AP/Wide World Photos, 42
© Bettmann/ CORBIS, 38
© Bob Daemmrich/ CORBIS, 50, 56
© Brooks Craft/ CORBIS, 65
© CORBIS, 14, 18, 22
© CORBIS Sygma, 21, 28, 34, 52
© Getty Images, 31, 88
© Greenhaven, 76, 82

© Joseph Sohm; ChromoSohm Inc./ CORBIS, 62
© Landov, 10, 11, 41, 79
© Reuters NewMedia Inc./ CORBIS, 9, 45, 87
© Reynaldo Ramon/U.S. Air Force/ CORBIS, 94
© Ron Sachs/Corbis, 91
© Rykoff Collection/ CORBIS, 27

About the Authors

Rose Blue, a native New Yorker who lives in Brooklyn, has published more than eighty fiction and nonfiction books for children. Two of her books were adapted for young people's specials aired by the NVC television network.

Corinne J. Naden, a former children's book editor and U.S. Navy journalist, has written more than eighty books for young people and lives in Tarrytown, New York.

CD

CODMAN SQUARE